MW00877499

Kingdom of Nain

Dr. Christine Le

Book design and illustrations by Michel Lê
Edited by Samantha Lê
Author photo by Charlotte Lê

For contact and comments, please visit the author's page at www.facebook.com/author.christine.le

First printing, April 2013

May God bless you.

To the Father
I lift this book up to you.
Thank you for entrusting me with it.

and to

Michel
Who helped lead me onto a path that is true.

Table *of* Contents

1

Alone in the Mud

Elisha's amazing adventure began on April 12th, a day that was just like any other. At the first recess, she put on the orange Junior Police Officer jacket, picked up the clipboard with the list of things that kids were not supposed to do, and walked outside.

A group of girls were huddled together with Nicole, the tallest of them all, in the center. She was handing out invitations to a party. Elisha watched, as the large pile of envelopes became smaller and smaller, and for just one moment she thought she might be given one. But then Nicole stretched out her hand with the last one in it, and gave it to someone else.

Elisha looked down at the clipboard. Item number five on the list was the only reason she did yard duty. She loved to call out number five. So she headed over to the field where the boys were kicking a soccer ball around.

Mark ran past. He was covered in mud, and his jeans were hanging down.

"Sagging pants," she shouted.

He stopped and turned around, face red. He pulled his jeans up, and took a ticket from her with his muddy fingers. "That's your second one this week," she scolded. "If you get one more you'll have detention."

"Stay away from me," he grunted. "Why don't you go hang out with the other girls?" She thought about this for a moment. It was true, she was usually by herself.

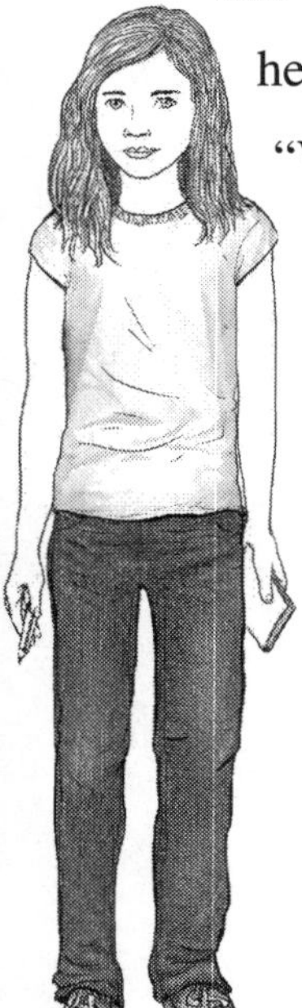

"What you need is a best friend," he said, running away.

And that's when it all started. Elisha, standing alone on the soccer field, feet now covered in mud, realized that she needed a friend.

2

A Miracle

The following Sunday Elisha opened the cereal and poured some into her bowl. It was not a good day for finding a best friend. Her family always went to church on Sunday, and she would be in the youth room. She shook the cereal harder. There was supposed to be a surprise inside.

"Hey," shouted her younger sister, Angela. "You're not going to eat all that. You just want the toy."

Her mom turned around. Cereal was spilling out of the bowl and onto the table, and she hadn't even poured the milk in yet. "I hope you're hungry," her mom muttered. Elisha narrowed her eyes into her famous stink eye look, and she turned towards her sister. Today was not going to be a good day.

The youth room was filled with all the usual kids. Nicole was organizing the worksheets for the lesson.

She was smiling and talking, and always seemed so full of energy and happy to be at church.

"Here you are," Nicole said. "Pastor John will be coming in a moment."

"Thanks," Elisha mumbled, taking the worksheet, not at all interested. She wished she could be somewhere else, like giving out tickets for the yard duty. But then she saw what was written on the top of the paper:

Making God Your Best Friend

Elisha ran up to Nicole to get a pencil. She quickly wrote her name in the corner of the page.

"Wonderful to see you working so hard," pastor John said from behind her. She usually tried to hide from him, hoping he wouldn't call on her. But today she felt different, she wanted to know about making a friend.

She looked down at the question on her sheet. 'How is God your best friend?' She didn't understand, she thought that this was going to tell her how to make friends with God, not ask her questions. She wrote down, "I don't know." All the other kids were writing. Nicole had even finished half a page.

Pastor John smiled at Elisha, a warm smile, and she knew that meant he was going to call on her. She felt embarrassed and tried to think of something to say.

"Okay Elisha, why don't you share what you wrote?" She sat there silent. "Did you write down what we learned last week?" She hadn't even listened to what he had said last week. "Don't be shy, we are all here to help each other."

Help, she needed more than help. She needed a miracle.

"Pastor John," a woman suddenly shouted from the doorway. "You're needed right away. I know you're good with animals, and a bird is trapped in the clock tower."

The pastor put his paper down. "Come on Elisha, you can come and tell me your answer on the way."

Elisha didn't have a chance to talk about what she had written. Instead, the pastor told her how the clock tower was the tallest building in the church, and the large clock at the top had never broken before. Then the woman said how the bird was making an awful noise, and no one knew how it had got into the building as the windows of the tower had been closed for years.

The bird was a large white dove, with the longest wings Elisha had ever seen, and a fan like tail. Several people were jumping around in the dimly lit room trying to catch it.

"Now, now," said pastor John. "You'll never bring it to you that way. You'll frighten it. Let's open the tower door and be very still. Then it will fly towards the light."

A gray haired man pushed the door open as wide as it would go. The dove turned its head towards the light, as if thinking about moving. "It's working," whispered the woman, and everyone shuffled to the side to give the bird space to fly out. It was then that Elisha saw a narrow staircase winding up to the top of the tower. She curiously crept past the woman. First one step, then another, creaking higher and higher. It wasn't like anyone had said she couldn't go. Finally she came to the last step. She was very high up and could hear the bird below. She was in a small room, standing at the back of the clock. Daylight came through the face of the clock, giving it a yellow glow. From where she was standing the hands on the clock were back to front, but she could see that it was five minutes to twelve.

Elisha almost left the room without seeing it, but then she looked down and noticed a wooden box on the floor. It was covered in dust, and there was some writing on the lid. She knelt down next to it, wiped the dust off, and saw the words ***secret prayer.*** She opened the lid. Inside was a blank piece of paper and a pencil.

Elisha knew exactly what to do. If God was going to be her best friend she needed to meet him first, and she didn't mean once she had died. She wanted to meet him now. So she picked up the paper and pencil and wrote 'I pray to meet God.' She put the paper and pencil back in the box and closed the lid.

The clock started to strike twelve. Dong. It was very loud. She covered her ears. Then suddenly the room started to get brighter. Dong. Light was pouring out of the box, filling the room. Dong. So bright she couldn't see anything anymore. The box, the clock, the tower, all disappeared. Then the sound of the clock started to fade. She took her hands off her ears. Everything was quiet. Peaceful. The light began to fade too.

And instead of the clock, and the tower, and the room, she was sitting in the middle of a beautiful green valley. And someone was standing over her.

3

Faith

She didn't think God would look quite like that. She had expected an old man with a beard, but the someone standing in front of her was tall with long orange hair flowing wildly in the wind. He had a big smile, large round eyes, and four fingers on each hand. He looked like a tall, thin troll. Elisha thought that trolls were short and lived under bridges.

"Hello," the someone said, stretching out his hand. She stared at the four fingers. "Oh, it's okay," he said, guessing her thoughts. "You shake hands the same way as with five fingers. You'll get used to it."

She shook his hand. "Hi God."

The someone started laughing, his orange hair standing straight up now, shaking, as if it were laughing too. "Sorry, but I'm not God."

Elisha was secretly happy that God was not a troll.

He smiled at her kindly. "You can call me Someone."

"Angel Someone," she said.

He lowered his voice, "Well, I'm not an actual angel."

Elisha looked disappointed. He wasn't God. He wasn't an angel. Who was he? Then he said, "I can't do everything that the angels can."

"Like what?"

He looked up at the sky as if the clouds had something to do with it. "If you want to call me Angel Someone, I'm sure God wouldn't mind." Elisha smiled and he continued, "He likes the angels to protect and guide people. And I know I do that."

"You can help guide me?" she said, looking around the valley, wondering where she was.

"Of course I can," he replied. He waved his hand across the land, "Let me tell you where you are. This, is the Kingdom of Nain." He picked up a trumpet and blew several short bursts.

Elisha heard a loud flapping sound coming from above. She looked up and saw a great winged creature flying towards them.

Its golden fur was as bright as the sun, so she shielded her eyes as it came closer. It landed right next to them and she saw that it had the body of a lamb, and four large wings. "Where to?" the lamb asked.

"Angel Gabriel's field," he said. Angel Someone climbed on its back, and then he held out his hand for Elisha to climb on too.

The lamb started to rise and Elisha closed her eyes tight. "Don't you want to look?" the angel asked. Elisha tried to open one eye, but now they were far above the ground, above the tree tops, above the hills. She slid her hands deep into the soft golden curls and held on tight.

Angel Someone put his arms up into the air. "You can't fall off. It's impossible."

"Well I could slip, or the lamb could suddenly go upside down."

"Can you fall from the earth?" he asked.

"Of course not," Elisha answered, annoyed now.

"Well you can't fall off the lamb either." This seemed very strange to Elisha and she held on even tighter. "What you need is faith," he said.

"Faith?"

"Yes. Faith is when you believe in something you can't see." Elisha became very quiet. It was true, she didn't have much faith. For her to believe in something she needed to see it and touch it. Her teacher was always saying she needed to have faith in her work. But until she saw the 'A' on her paper, she didn't believe she could do it.

"Well since you lack faith, I'm just going to have to show you." Then the angel leapt from the lamb into the sky.

"No," Elisha shouted. "Don't."

Angel Someone's orange hair trembled as he fell down, down, towards the land. Elisha half covered her eyes so that she was watching through her fingers. He was getting smaller, further away. A tiny dot about to crash. But then she saw that his falling slowed, and then stopped. He floated for a moment in one place, and the strangest thing happened. He began to float upwards, away from the ground towards the lamb, as if he was on a giant elastic band.

He landed on the lamb's back. "Hi," he said, smiling. It was true, you couldn't fall off.

By the time they were over Gabriel's field, Elisha had enough faith to put both hands into the air. And she was flying with her arms raised high above her head when they went into the rainbows. Hundreds of them, covering Gabriel's field.

Elisha had never stood next to a rainbow before. She had seen them stretched over the mountains near her house, and double ones hanging in the sky on a rainy summer's day, but whenever she had tried to get close to them they seemed to move. Now her whole body was covered in multicolored stripes.

"All the rainbows are kept in Gabriel's field," Angel Someone said. "We try to sort them by size, small ones in the front, large ones in the back, but they're always getting muddled up." He stretched out his arms to measure one. "I think this one needs moving," he said. He blew on it, and the rainbow started to slide down the row. "I'll need to go with it," he shouted, running away. "Just wait here, Angel Gabriel will be arriving soon."

Elisha had a purple stripe on one arm, a yellow stripe on the other, and she was just about to move her right leg into blue when she heard a deep calm voice say, "Hi. I'm Angel Gabriel." She quickly jumped out of the rainbow. "Oh, don't worry," he assured her. "I play in them all the time."

"Angel Gabriel?" she asked, staring at his jeans, t-shirt, and shoes. He didn't look like an angel at all. Then she noticed his eyes. They sparkled with light and wisdom, like an ancient star that shone through the night sky. She then knew that she could trust him.

"Oh no," he said. "Not again. I always forget to wear my angel outfit." He glanced over to a long white robe, golden wings, and a halo hanging against a tree. "You would think I'd remember. I've welcomed so many in the last two thousand years."

"You're two thousand years old?"

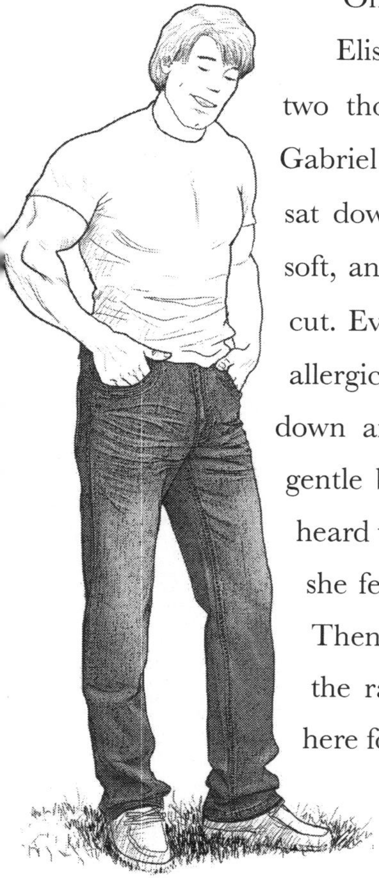

"Oh much, much older," he muttered.

Elisha couldn't imagine being over two thousand years old. Then Angel Gabriel sat down on the grass, and she sat down next to him. The grass was soft, and smelled as if it had just been cut. Even though Elisha was normally allergic, she wasn't itchy at all. She laid down and closed her eyes. She felt a gentle breeze, and in the distance she heard the sound of a river flowing, and she felt as if she was floating with it. Then she opened her eyes, and saw the rainbows dancing. "I could stay here forever," she thought.

"So you prayed to meet God?" Angel Gabriel suddenly asked. Elisha sat up. She had forgotten all about her prayer. She had forgotten about the clock tower, the box, and everything.

"Do you still want to meet him?"

If Angel Gabriel hadn't asked the question, she might never have remembered. "Yes," she said. "I still want to meet him."

Angel Gabriel's face became serious. "There are many secrets in this kingdom," he whispered. "Things that even some adults do not know."

"What kind of secrets?"

He was silent. Then he said, "First we need to do some gardening."

"Gardening?" Elisha asked, thinking the angels were very strange.

He took an envelope out of his pocket, and handed it to her. On the outside was written FRUIT TREES. She opened it up and found tiny green seeds. "Could you plant these for me?" he asked kindly. "And be careful with them. Each seed is as valuable as God's teachings."

Elisha walked across the field until she came to a narrow path. She scattered the seeds onto the path.

"Watch out," said Angel Gabriel. "You're stepping on them." Some of the seeds were stuck to the bottom of her shoes. She brushed them off.

Elisha continued down the path until the envelope was empty. The path was now covered in tiny seeds, and she was excited to think of all the fruit trees that would grow. But just as she was about to ask Angel Gabriel if he thought she had done a good job, a black and red bird landed near her feet. It looked directly at her, flapped its wings, and ate some of the seeds.

"Oh dear, oh dear," said Angel Gabriel. "Those seeds didn't last long."

Then the bird made a high pitched call and others arrived. They flew all over the path, and started to snatch the seeds away. In less than a minute all of the seeds were gone.

Elisha sat down on the empty path. "It's all my fault," she said.

"Small seeds are so easily destroyed," replied Angel Gabriel sadly.

Elisha turned to look at him. "I didn't even plant them," she said. "I just scattered them all over the place."

Angel Gabriel put his hand on his heart. "It takes

great care to make a seed grow."

And suddenly Elisha remembered. God had planted an idea in her heart: To be his friend. The idea was new and small like the seeds. She needed to take good care of it, so that it could grow.

"The secrets you were talking about. Will they help me meet God?" she asked.

Angel Gabriel smiled, "You remembered your prayer. God will be happy, and all the secrets of the kingdom will be given to you."

When Elisha heard these words she felt her heart jump with excitement. Angel Gabriel was very old and not at all what she would have expected, but she knew he was there to help. He smiled at her, and before she could reply, the winged lamb was diving down towards them like a falling star.

"It will take you to the far corner of the field," Angel Gabriel said. Elisha climbed on its back and rose into the sky. Angel Gabriel called up to her from below. "Look for the golden jar at the end of the rainbow."

4

Into Blue

When Elisha first saw the brown paper in the jar she felt disappointed. She had expected gold. But then she remembered her prayer. She had been given money before, dollar notes on her birthday, and they had never helped her to meet God.

The paper was rolled up like a scroll. She took it slowly out of the jar and unrolled it. Inside there was a message:

To find your way you need God's light
Especially in the dark of night
Just put the scroll into blue
And write down all you should not do

Elisha read the message several times. God's light. Dark of night. It wasn't dark. The sun was shining brightly, and from where she was standing, she couldn't see any clouds. Into blue. She had no idea where she was supposed to put the scroll.

After thinking about it for a while, she decided to look for a blue mailbox. She walked up one side of the field. Then down the other. She looked in the long grass, and up the trees. But all she could see were rainbows. And then Elisha started to read the scroll again, and just as she was getting to the last part 'all you should not do,' she noticed that the wind had become stronger and that the rainbows were dancing more. Some yellow went onto the scroll.

"Into blue," she shouted, putting the scroll into the blue of the rainbow. And as she held it there the blue got brighter and brighter. So bright that the field and the rainbows, and the Kingdom of Nain disappeared. All that was left was blue.

Then the light began to fade and she heard a familiar sound. Dong. She was standing behind the clock in the tower, and the time on the clock was twelve.

It was only because Elisha was still holding the scroll that she believed it had all happened. Without it, she might have thought that she had fallen asleep, or imagined it in her head.

"I don't think the bird's going to move," she heard the pastor say from below. "We'll try again later."

Elisha rolled up the scroll and crept back down the stairs. The bird was now sitting on top of a window frame, far from the door. She walked past it, and it flapped its wings as if excited. "It seems to like you," the pastor said. "Maybe next time you can ask it to leave." Elisha looked up at the bird and it seemed to wink at her.

"I'm sure it will be gone in a couple of days," one of the older women said.

"I hope so," said the pastor. "We need this room to store the bake sale cookies. It's just the right size, and nice and cool."

Elisha hoped that it would never leave, so that the clock tower door would always be open, and she could return to the Kingdom of Nain.

By the time the pastor and Elisha got back to the youth room, the others had finished the worksheet and were talking about what they were going to make for the church bake sale.

"Can we meet some other time?" the pastor asked Elisha. "I really want to hear your ideas about making God your best friend."

"Sure," said Elisha, feeling a little better now that she had the scroll to help her. Then she added, "I know that making God your best friend takes great care. Like planting seeds. If you don't take care of them the birds will come and eat them up."

"You're absolutely right," said the pastor, his eyes shining like Angel Gabriel's. "Can I share that in one of my sermons?"

Elisha nodded. At last she was starting to understand some things about God.

On Monday, Elisha took the scroll to school, hoping to find out more about what the poem meant. She knew that she had to write down everything that she should not do, but she wasn't too sure what that meant exactly. Did it mean the school rules, like the ones on her yard duty paper?

At recess she stayed in the class instead of going outside. Her teacher, Ms. Judd was at her desk grading papers. Elisha took the scroll out of her bag. She read,

"Write down all you should not do."

"What did you say Elisha?" Ms. Judd asked.

Elisha hadn't realized she'd been reading out loud. She stared silently at her teacher for what seemed like a very long time.

Then all she could think of to say was, "I was wondering if you've graded my math."

Ms. Judd smiled, and pulled a paper out of the pile. "Here you are Elisha. You can have it now if you like."

Elisha went up to Ms. Judd. Her paper had a red circle around one of the problems, and a large 'A' at the top. "You did really well. Just one thing you should not have done," Ms. Judd said. "You shouldn't have . . ."

And then Elisha did not hear anything else Ms. Judd said. All she could do was stare at the red circle. That's what the scroll meant. The things you should not do were like the mistakes on her math test, only they were mistakes that she knew were wrong. Things that were bad. Things that she shouldn't do, but she did anyway, like cheating on her homework, or lying.

God wanted her to change her bad ways. Maybe God was a teacher too.

"Thanks Ms. Judd. You're the best," Elisha said.

Ms. Judd smiled. "You're welcome. I didn't realize you were so interested in your math test." Elisha took the math paper and skipped out of the room. "You can come anytime for extra help," she heard Ms. Judd call out.

The next day Elisha carried the scroll with her everywhere she went. She wrote down all the bad things she was doing.

7:00 a.m. Took too much cereal (didn't find the toy!).

7:30 a.m. Picked nose in car, flicked booger at back of mom's seat (it fell on the floor).

8:15 a.m. Hid eraser shavings in desk.

9:20 a.m. Used toilet paper, water, and soap to make spit balls in the bathroom.

10:00 a.m. Followed Mark all recess (no luck giving him a ticket).

10:45 a.m. Used class time to make putty from eraser shavings.

12:30 p.m. Went to bathroom to check on spit balls (They were still on ceiling!)

3:00 p.m. Faked doing homework.

3:50 p.m. Told after school director homework was done.

4:00 p.m. Hugged dad when he came to pick me up (so I could wipe my nose on him).

Her last bad deed had left a two inch streak on the side of her dad's shirt, but he hadn't seemed to notice. He was too busy talking to Nicole's dad about how much bread to bake for the church sale.

Elisha took out the scroll and added: 4:10 p.m. Gave dad stink eye for talking too long when I wanted to go home. She had just written the word 'home' when a voice behind her asked, "What are you doing?"

Elisha turned around. Nicole was standing right next to her staring at the scroll. Elisha's heart gave a little leap of fear, and she slammed her hands on top of the scroll to try to cover it up, but her list was too long and her fingers too short to hide it all. She couldn't tell anyone what had happened.

"Looks really ancient," Nicole said.

"Ancient?"

"Yes, you know, really old. It looks really old."

Elisha nodded, and slid her fingers so that now all of the poem was showing. Maybe Nicole could help.

Nicole started to read the poem out loud, and when she got to the "all you should not do" she suddenly shouted "That's great. I did that once."

"You did?" Elisha took her hands all the way off the scroll.

"Sure, it's called making a list of your sins. Pastor John talks about it all the time."

Sins. That sounded like a bad word to Elisha. Like she would be grounded for a month. And her list was very long. Maybe she would be grounded for two months.

"Only thing is," Nicole said, sliding her finger along each item on the list, "you've forgotten to put down the stuff you did wrong before today. Like the things you did wrong last week, and the week before that."

"You mean everything?" Elisha whispered, afraid that someone else might hear.

"Well everything you can think of. Like how you're

always teasing your little sister." Elisha felt like she was going to cry. Surely God wouldn't want to be her friend once he saw something like that.

"You're doing a good job," Nicole said softly, as if she could see that Elisha was getting upset. "A few more things and you'll be done."

"Thanks," Elisha said, sorry that she had ever let Nicole see it. Sorry that she had ever found the Kingdom of Nain.

"You can do it," Nicole said, and she handed her a blue lollipop. Elisha stared at the color and it reminded her of the rainbow field, and Angel Gabriel, and Angel Someone.

Elisha closed her eyes and imagined that she was riding on the back of the golden lamb, arms stretched in the air, certain that she could not fall. Then she picked up her pencil and began to write.

5

God's Light

By the time she got home, Elisha had written down everything she could think of. Everything except being mean to her little sister. God would be angry if he saw that. Besides, she had almost filled the scroll up. There was only one empty line left.

She pushed open the front door and the smell of fresh bread came flowing out. She imagined herself eating a thick slice with melting butter on top. Her sister, Angela, was piling several loafs into a basket.

"Five minutes and the last ones should be done," her mom said, peering into the oven. Then she picked up a slice of bread with melting butter. "You've been such a help Angela," she said, handing it to her. Angela gave Elisha an

‘I’m the good one’ look.

“Can I have some mom?” Elisha asked.

“Sorry, that’s the last slice. The rest is for the church.”

“Mom.”

“Well maybe I can make more tomorrow.”

Elisha knew she wouldn’t make more the next day. That was just a fancy way of saying no. So she turned around and gave her sister the dirtiest look she could.

When they arrived at church, Elisha insisted on waiting outside. “But it’s getting dark,” her mom said, “and you know you love to decorate the room for the bake sale.” Her mom was right, she usually loved to put up the balloons and streamers, but today she felt different. Something wasn’t right. She sat down on the garden wall. “Well if you change your mind,” her mom coaxed, pointing to the room.

Elisha took out the scroll. The empty line was still there, as if it was waiting to be filled. She looked down her list again, but the sun had started to set, and the light was fading. She wondered if the clock tower door was open. Maybe she could just take the scroll back.

She stood up and started to walk along the path, but now it was very dark, and she couldn't see where she was going. The building next to her looked strange, and her heart told her she had gone the wrong way.

She stared into the dark. She felt alone, and she began to worry that she might not find the right path. How could she have got lost so easily? She thought she was good at directions. She had even helped others who were lost. Maybe she had sent them the wrong way too. She zipped up her jacket and continued on. The night was getting colder. The light dimmer. Was this what the poem meant by 'the dark of night?' It was not a nice place to be. But then, just when she thought there was no hope of finding where she wanted to go, she began to notice two small lights beaming through the dark, and she heard the faint sound of a bicycle bell. The lights became brighter and brighter as they got closer, and she heard two men talking. She recognized one of the voices as pastor John's.

"Over here!" she shouted. "It's me Elisha." The bicycles stopped right next to her. Pastor John jumped off, and his bike fell over.

"Elisha, are you okay?" he asked.

"I got lost." Her voice was quiet and trembling. "I was going to the clock tower, and then it got dark."

"You must have made a wrong turn back there," he said, pointing into the shadows. "But I'm happy we found you." Then he turned towards the man on the other bicycle. "Oh, I'm sorry. This is pastor Gilbear. He's visiting from France."

The pastor smiled, and even though it was too dark to see his face clearly, Elisha thought he looked very familiar. "Have we met before?" she asked.

Pastor Gilbear just continued to smile. "He's an old friend of mine from Paris," pastor John said, "and he's excellent at baking." Elisha noticed his bicycle basket was full of all different types of loafs: round ones, square ones, white, and brown ones. He must have been baking for days.

Pastor John picked up his bicycle. Then he bent over and started fiddling with the chain. "It's come off," he said. "Do you mind waiting a moment while I fix it?"

"Of course not," pastor Gilbear said. "Maybe God wanted it to come off."

"Well yes, he might have," replied pastor John.

"Why would he want to do that?" Elisha asked. "Why would he want to go around breaking things?" She felt sorry for pastor John, who was now turning his whole bicycle upside down to get the chain back on, and his hands were all black with grease.

"We just see the broken bicycle," pastor Gilbear said. "So of course we think it's a bad thing. But God sees everything. He sees the whole plan. Maybe the bicycle breaking is part of his plan."

"He sees everything?" Elisha asked.

"Yes. He sees the past, the present, and the future. He knows when you sit and when you rise, when you go out and when you lay down. He knew you even before you were born. And he is with you now. He hears every word you speak, and he hears the words hidden in your heart. He even knows the exact number of hairs on your head." Then pastor Gilbear glanced down at Elisha's bag, and she remembered the scroll.

If God had counted the number of hairs on her head, he would know that she had been mean to her little sister. And the empty line was still waiting to be filled.

"Can I ask you something?" Elisha said in a very quiet voice.

"Anything you like," pastor Gilbear replied. "I've been sent to this church to help everyone who wants to be closer to God."

Elisha hesitated. She looked at pastor Gilbear's eyes and saw a warmth in them, and she felt a courage growing inside her heart. Then she thought she knew the answer to her question even before she asked, but she asked it anyway.

"If I'm making a list of my . . ." she hesitated for a moment not wanting to say the word. "Sins," she continued. "Will God be angry at me if some of those things are mean things?"

Pastor Gilbear bent down to Elisha's height, and put his hand gently on her shoulder. He smiled, softly. And just these movements, his looking at her like that, told her it was okay.

"God loves you," he said. "He wants to be your friend too."

"He does?" she asked. "Even with all my sins."

"Yes. Even with all of them." Elisha felt a great joy

rising up inside her, she pulled out the scroll, and sat down on the ground in front of the small bicycle light, and in the empty line she added:

Was also mean to my little sister.

"Look," pastor Gilbear said, pointing to a full moon sliding out from behind a cloud. The light shone brightly on the paper, and Elisha could now see the list clearly. She no longer wanted to hide it, and she was no longer afraid of being grounded. Instead, it felt good to be looking at her mistakes. She now knew what she needed to fix.

"God's light," pastor Gilbear said.

Elisha closed her eyes, and even though the light was from the moon and not the sun, she felt a warmth on her body. She felt peaceful and calm. She felt as if she was meeting God for the very first time.

She opened her eyes. Then the moon came out all the way, and the path that had been dark before was now bathed in a silvery light. She could see her way clearly. She saw the church, the trees, and the clock tower that was just a few steps to her right. She had missed it in the dark. But now she could see. And the clock tower door was open.

Pastor Gilbear noticed her looking at the door. "I guess it's time for you to go," he said.

"Time for us to go as well," said pastor John, turning his bicycle the right way up. He gave the wheel a short spin with his hand, and the chain moved smoothly.

Maybe God did sometimes have to break things to help people. If the chain hadn't come off she wouldn't have had the chance to talk to pastor Gilbear. She wouldn't have filled in the empty line.

"God sees the whole plan," pastor Gilbear repeated, as if hearing her thoughts. Then he peered into his bicycle basket and pulled out a round loaf of bread. "Take this with you. It will feed many."

The bread was still warm, and it smelled as if it had just come out of the oven. And he handed her a small cup of butter and a plastic knife.

Elisha cut a slice for each of them, and spread the butter on top. It was the most amazing bread she had ever eaten.

"Thank you," she said, putting the rest into her bag, "Thank you for everything." The scroll was complete. She was ready to return to the Kingdom of Nain.

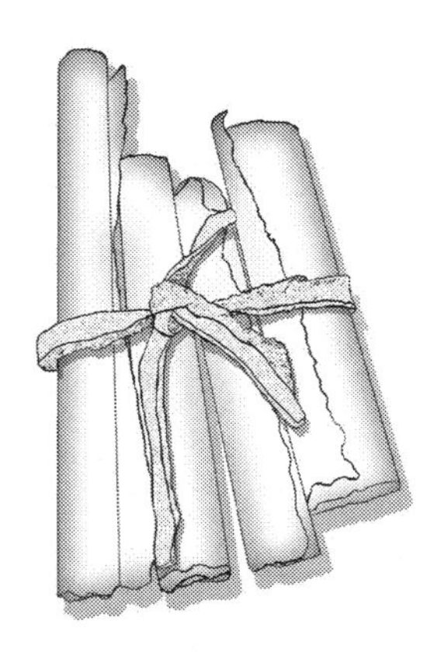

6

Digging Deeper

When Elisha entered the clock tower, she didn't see any baskets of cookies, only empty tables and a notice saying 'Put your baked goods here.' The dove was asleep in the corner.

She walked slowly up the stairs to the room at the top, the wooden floor creaking under her feet. The small box with the words ***secret prayer*** was still on the floor, and she opened it up expecting to find the prayer that she had written about wanting to meet God, but the paper inside was blank. She sat for a few minutes, wondering what to do. And then she took out the paper and pencil and wrote 'I pray to take my sins to the Kingdom of Nain.'

Even though Elisha had already visited the Kingdom, she noticed that her hands were shaking, and she wondered if her prayer would be answered, if she could return. She waited. She watched. The second hand on the clock moved around and around. She listened to the rhythm of the tick, tick, tick. Then gradually, her attention began to drift away from these things, and onto the same warm feeling that she had felt on the path. And she knew that God was with her. A light filled the room, and it grew brighter and brighter until everything disappeared. She looked down at the floor and she couldn't even see her feet. Then the light began to fade.

She was sitting on the path that led to the rainbows, bread crumbs were scattered all over, and there was a bicycle propped up against one of the trees. It had a basket on the front just like the pastor from France, and it was full of crumbs.

"Welcome back. Welcome back," Angel Gabriel called out cheerfully from the other end of the path. He was wearing a long white robe, golden wings, and there was a halo floating over his head. "I can fly too," he said, and his wings began to flap and he lifted a few feet into the air. Then he bumped his head on the branch of a tree and fell back to the ground.

"Forgotten how to fly," he muttered, rubbing his head.

"You look like . . ."

"An angel?" he asked. Elisha nodded. "People expect us to look this way," he continued. "That's why I keep the old outfit around."

"But you don't wear it anymore?"

Angel Gabriel laughed. "Well I can't wear it on earth."

Then suddenly, as if he had said something wrong, Angel Gabriel looked away. "Now, there's a beautiful rainbow," he said, pointing in the sky.

He was right, it was beautiful, but something was suspicious. "So you come down to earth?" Elisha asked.

Angel Gabriel didn't answer, but just continued to study the rainbow. Then, completely changing the subject he whispered, "Did you discover the first secret?"

Elisha thought that maybe Angel Gabriel was the one hiding a secret, but for now it would have to wait. She took the scroll out of her bag. "I discovered that God loves me," she said opening up her long list of sins. "Even with everything I've done wrong, he still wants to be my friend."

"Oh well done," said Angel Gabriel, flapping his wings so that he started to float up again, but this time covering his head with his hands. He peered over her shoulder to look at the list. "Yes, these are all your sins, all the things that God wants you to change. You even have your sister on there."

"And I met God," Elisha said.

"You did? What did he say?"

"Well, he didn't speak, but he gave me this feeling inside my heart, and I felt him shining down light from the moon that made my body warm."

"That's God's light," Angel Gabriel said. "That's definitely him. You can be wandering around in the dark, not knowing whether to go this way or that. Then his light will shine, and everything is clear. Like you can see again."

Elisha jumped up with excitement. "That's just what happened."

"Well then, that's definitely him."

Elisha had learned the first secret to meeting God. She knew how to make a list of her bad deeds, and how not to be afraid to show them to him. She knew that

God loved her, even though she wasn't perfect.

Angel Gabriel had said that there were many secrets to learn. But she had met God after only learning the first one. She didn't need to discover the rest.

She looked over at the rainbows for one last time, and putting the scroll back in her bag, she said, "I think I can go home now."

Angel Gabriel smiled gently. Then he asked, "Before you go could you do me one favor?"

"Sure."

"Would you help me plant these seeds?"

He showed her a small packet exactly the same as the last one, except this time on the outside were the words, MORE FRUIT TREES. Angel Gabriel really seemed to like gardening. She hadn't been that good at it the last time, and she was surprised he had asked her again. But it was a small favor to ask, and now she knew that she had to plant them in the soil so the birds couldn't snatch them away.

Elisha walked along the path until she found the perfect spot. On her right was a hill covered in rich dark soil. She took the envelope from Angel Gabriel and opened it. "I'll be back later," he said, and he flapped his wings and floated off into the sky like a disappearing balloon.

Elisha dug her hands into the damp soil. It was perfect for planting. She made tiny holes with her fingers, and dropped the seeds in one by one, careful to cover them up. She didn't step on any of the seeds, and the birds stayed far away. She worked hard, covering the whole hill. Then just as she was finishing, Angel Gabriel dove out of the sky on the back of the Golden Lamb.

"Not using your wings?" she laughed.

"Well, the Golden Lamb can carry us both. Come on, we're going to the rainbows."

Elisha climbed on, and she let her body drop so that only her thumb was touching the lamb's ear. She had no fear of falling. Only faith that the lamb would carry her. They flew up one side of a rainbow, and then down the other. They zigzagged in and out of green and blue, as a hot breeze made the rainbows dance.

Then Elisha climbed back on, and Angel Gabriel jumped from the lamb towards a tall archway made of vines. "Follow me," he called to Elisha as he floated under the green leaves. "This is the only way to get where you want to go."

Elisha stared at him, puzzled, wondering if she could just go around it. The lamb, sensing her hesitation flew in place, waiting. She didn't even know where they were going. And she was just about to ask the angel if he could show her a map, when she suddenly surprised herself by shouting out "Okay," and the lamb and Elisha dived through.

Angel Gabriel climbed back on. "We should go back and check the seeds now," he smiled.

"Now?" Elisha questioned. "I only just planted them."

"Things grow differently here," he told her. "Why, sometimes a whole tree can grow in a day."

No wonder Angel Gabriel liked gardening. The trees might even have fruit on them by now. Elisha imagined herself walking under their shade, knowing that she was the one who had planted them. "Let's pick some fruit for Angel Someone," she said.

And then Elisha saw the hill where she had planted the seeds. There was no fruit. No trees. No branches. No trunks. Only shriveled plants about six inches high. The tops of the plants were bent over, and small leaves curled

on thin stalks as if they had given up trying to grow. Elisha ran up to one of the plants. "What happened?" she shouted. She wanted to help them, but she could see it was too late. These trees would never have fruit.

Angel Gabriel dug deep around the plant, revealing the roots. "Look," he said, softly.

Elisha saw that the soil was only a few inches deep, and that under the soil was rock. The trees had started to grow, but when they had come to the stone the roots couldn't go any further. Without long roots, they hadn't had the water they needed to survive when the hot winds had blown.

"You are like these plants right now," Angel Gabriel said. "You are happy that you met God, and your faith has started to grow. But there are five secrets to learn, and without learning them all, your roots will be small and weak. You will have faith in God for a little while, but when a difficult day comes, you will wither up like these plants, never producing fruit."

Elisha held the plant in her hand. She felt the dried leaves, the weak stem. She didn't understand what Angel Gabriel meant by her producing fruit, but she knew that she didn't want to be like these trees. She needed long, strong roots. She needed to learn more.

She looked up at Angel Gabriel. "Can I have the second scroll?" she asked.

7

Bread of Life

Nobody noticed Elisha creeping back down the clock tower stairs. The small group of people gathered in the room below were too busy staring at the empty tables.

"I don't understand it," one woman said. "We always have baskets and baskets of cookies."

"Usually more cookies than bread," added another.

Pastor John bent down and looked under the table. "None here. I suppose no one baked any this year."

"No one?" the group of people repeated.

"No. No one. But with no food in here, at least we don't need to remove the bird."

The bird opened one of its eyes, as if knowing it was being talked about. Then it turned its head and looked directly at a tall pale man entering the doorway. He was dressed in a long black coat, black hat and boots, and was holding a pole with a net at the end. "Well I think we should get rid of it anyway," he said gruffly. "We can't leave the door open forever." He stepped forward, and swooped the net down towards the dove, missing it by only a few inches. "If we can get it, we can lock this place up."

Elisha gasped and the man turned towards her. "Locked up" he shouted at her, as if knowing that she needed to come back to the clock tower and the prayer box. He slammed the net down for a second time, and the edge of the net caught one of the bird's feathers. The bird fluttered, half trapped.

"Got it," he laughed. But then the bird fluttered some more and flapped its wings, and in one great movement it flew upwards, leaving only the trapped feather behind. It flew up the stairs, to the ceiling at the top of the tower.

"No more nets," pastor John said firmly to the man. "Best to be patient. It'll leave when it's ready."

"Or when I think of another way of getting it," the man called up the tower, as if challenging the bird.

Angel Gabriel had said there were five secrets to learn. If she was going to find them before the tower was locked up, she would have to hurry. She walked quickly over to the church hall, and saw that they were finishing the decorations.

"There you are," her mom said, giving her a big hug. "I was worried about you."

Her sister came running up. "Mom said you've been gone for over an hour."

Elisha looked at the time. She was sure she hadn't been lost on the path that long. Some time must have gone by when she was in the kingdom. That was why she hadn't heard the group of people coming into the clock tower. On her next visit she would need to be more careful. "Sorry mom," she said.

Then she pulled the bread out of her bag, keeping the first and second scrolls hidden inside. "Here, you can add this to the bake sale."

"What a wonderful loaf," her mom said. "Where did you get it?"

"From this new French pastor."

"Who?"

"Pastor Gilbear. He bakes, and he talked about how I want to be God's best friend."

Her mom looked surprised. "You want God to be your best friend?"

Elisha suddenly remembered that she hadn't told her mom about her adventures. In fact, the only person who knew anything was Nicole. And then she thought about the conversation with pastor Gilbear. How had he known that she wanted God to be her best friend? Had pastor John told him about the lesson in the youth room?

Elisha held on tightly to her bag with the scrolls. "Yes," she replied. "I want God to be my best friend."

That night in bed, Elisha opened up scroll number two. She flattened the scroll out carefully. Then, using her flashlight she read the message:

Even though I am known as the Son
My Father and I are really one
Over two thousand years since my birth
And my Spirit is still upon the earth

Two thousand years. Elisha remembered that Angel Gabriel had said that he had last worn his angel outfit about two thousand years ago. Elisha rolled up the scroll and turned off the flashlight. She closed her eyes. She would try to figure it out in the morning, it was late and she needed to sleep.

But her thoughts kept returning to the message. Two thousand years since my birth. My Spirit is still upon the earth. She pulled the bed covers up higher. And then her mind, with all these questions, drifted into a dream.

She was in the Kingdom of Nain, except there were no rainbows, only a river flowing down a long grassy hill. The water was pure, clear as crystal, and flowed rapidly over the rocks. Along the banks of the river, fruit trees were growing, and in the stream were hundreds of colorful fish. She approached the river, and when she looked carefully she saw that it was not one river, but three, flowing in and out of each other. Then she started to follow them, down great mountains and valleys. She danced between them, she stood at the points where they crossed each other letting the water flow over her feet. She saw that the fish moved easily between the streams. And wherever the waters flowed, the land became rich with fruits of all different kinds, and the animals from the smallest to the largest came near, and she thought she saw the Golden Lamb.

And then Elisha awoke. She felt peaceful. This was a good thing, because today was the bake sale.

She hurried into the kitchen where her sister was already at the breakfast table, studying the outside of the cereal box. "I'm going to find the toy today," Angela said smiling. Elisha's hand touched the side of the box, and without thinking, more by habit than anything else, she grabbed it before her sister could.

Elisha watched as her sister's smile faded, and as she

watched she saw something else. It wasn't just that Angela was sad about not getting the box, but it seemed that she was sad to have a mean sister. Elisha remembered the kind eyes of pastor Gilbear. She wanted to be kind in just the same way. She wanted to stop being mean.

She carried the cereal box over to her sister. "Let me help you. Maybe we can find the toy together." Her sister's face lit up, just like the darkened path had lit up with God's light. And Elisha felt that she had begun to turn in a new direction.

Elisha continued her new path all the way to the bake sale hall. No more sitting outside. She was going to help. She found the loaf of bread that pastor Gilbear had given her, and she cut some slices and put butter on top. "Warm bread and butter, just ten cents a slice."

A man came up and bought two slices. And it was only when she was handing it over to him that she realized that the bread was still warm from the night before. Was this possible? Or had pastor Gilbear come in and warmed it up? But then more people came and all she could think of was making slices, spreading the butter. And the jar of dimes got fuller and fuller.

Then all of a sudden pastor Gilbear was standing in front of her. She stopped slicing, and just stared at him feeling nervous. She looked down at the ground, and then back at him.

"People like the bread," he said.

Elisha put the butter back on the table. She shouldn't be surprised to see him. He was working at the church. He had given her the loaf.

"Yes," she replied, trying to make her voice sound calm. "It's been selling all morning." Then she looked at the loaf, and realized what it was that was troubling her. She had been selling the bread all morning, but the loaf hadn't got any smaller.

She didn't understand how this was happening, but she had the feeling that God had something to do with it. He was with her, and he wanted her to grow long, strong, roots. She pulled her bag out from under the table and took out scroll number two. "I'm looking for someone," she said, pointing to the message. "Can you help?"

The pastor smiled and came around to her side of the table so he could read the words. "The one you are looking for is also known as the bread of life. If you believe in him you will never be hungry."

"Never?"

Pastor Gilbear looked at the loaf and said, "He can feed many."

And then, before Elisha could ask any more, he walked back through the crowd and disappeared.

8

Rest in Me

Since the day of the bake sale Elisha had not been getting much rest. She had trouble doing her math. She had trouble doing her homework. Trouble sleeping. Trouble eating. And she knew that this wasn't what pastor Gilbear meant by never being hungry.

She needed God's help. So she spent her recesses outside, sitting in the warmth of the sun, looking at the green trees and the blue sky, and the way the petals on the flowers were shaped. She smelled the cut grass, and listened to the sounds of her classmates' voices drifting across the field. She watched a lady bug crawling along a bush, ten black dots painted on its red body. And she thought how good God was at making things.

And then, one day at first recess, an idea began to grow in her heart. To be close to God she needed to keep walking in her new direction.

At second recess, all dressed up in her Junior Police Officer jacket with her clipboard in her hand, she took a left onto the kindergarten playground instead of a right onto the soccer field. She was walking away from Mark, away from giving him a ticket every recess, away from trying to embarrass him in front of his friends.

She still longed to tease him, but now she knew it was not what God wanted. So she watched the children playing on the jungle gym, and then little by little she began to think less about Mark. She felt God's warmth upon her. And then she saw two girls arguing over a hula hoop.

"It's mine," the first girl shouted.

"No, I had it first. Give it back."

Elisha went over to talk to them about sharing, and while she was talking a strange thing happened. All of her thoughts drifted away from Mark, and she remembered that showing kids how to solve their recess problems was an important part of JPO. It was something she had forgotten to do. Eventually the two girls said sorry, and they skipped away together.

"Aren't you usually on the soccer field?" It was

Nicole, climbing out from under the slide with a shoe in her hand. A kindergarten boy hopped over to her, and he put the shoe back on.

"I was going to hop home," he said.

Both Elisha and Nicole smiled. Then Nicole looked closer at Elisha, stopped smiling, and said, "You look really tired. What happened?"

All of a sudden, Elisha's worries about not finding the answers to the second scroll came rising up inside her, and she couldn't speak. Then the bell rang. Nicole gave her a big hug. "Let's meet after school in the field next to the cafeteria."

After school they sat down on the grass in the shade of a large tree. Elisha pulled out scroll number two. "I have another message," she said. "I need to find out who this is. I showed it to pastor Gilbear and he said the person is also known as the bread of life, and I don't have much time. I need to learn five secrets, and once they get the bird out they're going to close the door."

Nicole had already begun reading. "Close the what?"

Elisha thought that maybe she had said too much. "I need to find out who this message is about," she said.

Nicole read the message out loud. "Even though I am known as the Son. My Father and I are really one. Over two thousand years since my birth. And my Spirit is still upon the earth." Nicole looked up with a sad expression in her eyes. "I don't understand," she said.

"No, I don't either."

"No, I mean, I understand who the poem is talking about. I know who it is."

"You do?" Elisha asked.

"Yes. But I don't understand why you don't know. You come to church all the time and pastor John is always teaching us about this." Nicole saw that Elisha looked hurt. She leaned close and said, "I'm sorry. "

And then Elisha thought about it, and the words that came out of her mouth surprised her. "Maybe I didn't want God to be my friend."

They sat silently for a moment and then Nicole asked, "But you do now?"

"Yes."

Nicole smiled and this encouraged Elisha. "I even started to meet God. I felt the warmth of his light, and he told me that it was okay that I made mistakes, and he lit up a path and showed me the way. And did you ever notice how good he is at making things?" Elisha picked a dandelion stalk out of the grass. "Look at how perfect this is."

On the top of the stem was a soft, round, circle of seeds. Elisha blew on it, and the seeds danced in the air until they landed on the ground. Nicole picked other flowers and blew on their seeds too, and soon the air was full.

Then Nicole said, "Did you know that God has walked on the earth?" Elisha's eyes opened up wide. "About two thousand years ago he came to visit. That's what the message is talking about."

"God? On the earth? Walking around?" Elisha had a hard time imagining this. She had a feeling that Angel Gabriel had come to the earth about two thousand years ago, but he had probably worn his angel outfit.

"What did he look like?" she asked.

"Like a normal person. Like you or me."

"Well, that's good," Elisha said seriously. "If he came looking like a big face in the cloud or something he'd probably scare people."

"Like that one?" Nicole asked, pointing through the branches to a cloud in the sky. It was oval shaped, with dark spots that looked like giant eyes, and a gray hole that made an angry mouth.

"Just like that," Elisha said. And then she whispered, "It's hard to believe that God would want to come to earth." She paused for a moment and asked, "What was his name?"

"Jesus," Nicole said. "His name's Jesus."

"Of course," Elisha shouted with excitement, sitting up. "Of course it's Jesus." Jesus had been born over two thousand years ago. And then she said softly, "I just never realized that Jesus was God."

"Well that's what the message is talking about. Jesus is called the Son, but he and God are really one."

Elisha looked confused. "So God made himself into a human?"

"Yep," said Nicole confidently.

"Are you sure?" Elisha asked. "Are you sure that Jesus is God?"

Nicole leaned forward. "I've been collecting proof. I did some experiments and have all sorts of evidence."

"Like what?"

Nicole was just about to answer, when Elisha's dad came walking out to the field. It was always like that, whenever he was early to pick her up, she was doing something important and wanted to stay.

"I have it all in a journal," Nicole said.

The next day, Nicole handed the journal to Elisha before first period, which happened to be math. Elisha

put the math book on top of her desk, and found the assignment on equilateral triangles. She completed the work quickly as she remembered that equilaterals had three sides the same length. So while others were still measuring all of the sides, she was sliding out the journal from underneath her desk.

On the front cover Nicole had written 'Very Very Private.' Elisha checked to make sure that no one was looking, and then she opened it up to the first page. She read:

This journal contains experiments done by me, Nicole. They are proof that God came to the earth and walked around as a human named Jesus. These experiments are super important.

Experiment 1:

DEAD THINGS

I found two dead ants and 1 dead cockroach. I put them in a box.

I checked them every day for a week but my dead things did not come back to life.

Jesus came back to life after being dead 3 days. Over 500 people saw him. He even ate some food. I don't think ghosts can eat food, so he must have been really alive.

ONLY GOD CAN DO THIS.

Experiment 2:

WHAT'S YOUR NAME?

What happens if you call someone important by the wrong name?

I called Principle Borris, Principle Beagle. He said "Nicole, my name's Borris not Beagle."

I called pastor John, pastor Jim. He said "Who's pastor Jim?"

I called Ms. Judd, Ms. Mud. She said "I hope you're not trying to be funny Nicole."

If you call someone important by the wrong name, they will say something about it.

Jesus was important. His friend Thomas called him God. Jesus did not tell him he was using the wrong name.

JESUS KNEW THAT HE WAS GOD.

Experiment 3:

MIRACLES

Using my own powers I tried to –

1. Make my teacher forget to give homework.
2. Get chosen for a free pizza party at Pizza Land.
3. Have a snow day in June.
4. Make my dead things come alive.

All of my miracles failed.

Jesus did lots and lots of miracles. I don't think he did them to show off, but because he wanted to help. I remember some of them. Jesus fed thousands of people with only five loafs of bread and two fish. Jesus walked on water. Jesus made a blind man see. Jesus made a dead boy alive again. Jesus stuck a man's ear back on after it was cut off.

ONLY GOD CAN DO ALL THIS.

Experiment 4:

Nothing was written underneath the last experiment. Perhaps Nicole hadn't finished writing everything down.

"Great experiments," Elisha said to Nicole at first recess. "It's true that nobody else has ever come back from the dead and been seen by five hundred people. And all the miracles he did. It must have been fun to hang out with Jesus."

Elisha handed the journal back. "What's experiment number four going to be?"

"I don't know, but I feel like there's one missing."

"Well, maybe you can just cross it out," Elisha suggested.

And for the rest of the day Elisha kept thinking how amazing it was that God had walked around on the earth. Jesus had been a child once just like her, so she knew he understood how hard it was sometimes. Then Elisha imagined what it must have been like to actually be with God, to sit down at a table and have a meal with him, to listen to him teach. She imagined the faces on the people when the dead son had stood up and started to speak.

Last summer her hamster had died and she had

buried him in the garden. What if Jesus had been there, had healed him, and the hamster had opened his eyes and scurried back to her? She imagined that her friends would not believe unless they had been there to see it.

And then she thought that there was some proof missing. Maybe Nicole needed one final experiment so that everyone, even those who hadn't been there at the time of Jesus, could know that Jesus was God.

The school bell rang and she went out to the shade of the tree. She laid down for a while watching the clouds. And as she watched, a feeling began to creep over her, a feeling that there was something else she needed to know. It crept slowly, like a vine creeping up a wall, so that at first she didn't even notice it, but then it grew stronger and stronger, until it was all that she could think about. She pulled out the scroll and read the message. She knew about God the Father. She now knew about Jesus the Son. But then she realized she didn't know about the Spirit. What was the Spirit upon the earth? It sounded like a ghost.

And then she felt herself say, "Please God show me this Spirit. I want to learn."

She sat up, and squinting into the sunlight she saw pastor Gilbear just a few feet away from her. He was walking past her classroom dressed in blue overalls, pushing the janitor's cart. She ran up to him. "What are you doing here?" she asked excitedly.

He turned around, and she realized it wasn't him, and she felt silly to be asking a stranger with a bucket and a broom, what he was doing at her school.

He smiled at her, a kind gentle smile, and simply said, "Spitballs."

Elisha knew exactly what he meant. He didn't need to say anymore. He had come to clean the spitballs off the bathroom ceiling. She had counted them the other day, there were twenty seven. Sixteen of them were hers. Every time she mashed up the water, paper and soap, and threw it at the ceiling, she made some extra work for someone.

And then, before she even had time to think about what she was saying, she picked up the broom and said, "I'll do it."

He smiled again, wider this time, so that his eyes were smiling too, and he handed her the stool. Soon Elisha was in the bathroom, standing on the stool, broom in hand. Who would have thought that knocking spitballs down was more fun then throwing them up?

And it was here, in the bathroom, pieces of soapy toilet paper in her hair, that she felt a gentle spirit growing in her heart. It was changing her from the inside out. It was warming her, showing her new things, like how wonderful it was to care about other people, to help others, to fix the mistakes she had made.

She thought about the message. The Father, he was God. She imagined him up in heaven, maybe with kind eyes and a beard. The Son, Jesus, he was God too, and he had come down to earth. And now it was like she was meeting the Spirit that was still upon the earth.

Jesus had died, but she felt as if she could still be with him, just like all those other people who had known him two thousand years ago. And the Spirit could be everywhere; with her, with Nicole, and with all of her family and friends. The Spirit could be there when she had dinner, or when she needed to fix her mistakes, like knocking down the spitballs. The Spirit could teach her, just like now. She could feel the Spirit in her heart, quietly telling her these things.

God was all three. He was the Father, the Son, and the Spirit. And then she felt God say to her "Holy Spirit, Elisha. The Holy Spirit."

She knocked the last spitball off the ceiling, swept them up, and went quickly outside. The man was gone, but the cart was still there, so she left the broom and stool and went running to find Nicole. She hoped she hadn't gone home yet.

"I know what experiment number four is," she said, as soon as she found Nicole in the cafeteria. "The final proof. I know what it is."

Nicole's face lit up, and Elisha continued. "The final proof will help you and teach you things, and change you. All you have to do is ask."

"Ask for what?"

"The Holy Spirit."

Nicole leaned closer. "You saw a Holy Spirit?"

"The Holy Spirit. And I didn't see a spirit exactly, but I think God put the Spirit into my heart, or maybe the Spirit was always in my heart and I didn't know. But I felt this warm feeling inside me, and it got stronger and stronger, and then I started to want to help people. I even went into the bathroom and knocked down the spitballs, and God began to teach me new things."

Nicole looked excited and said, "Pastor John told us that just before Jesus died, he said a counselor would be sent in his name. Counselors teach people. Counselors help and guide."

"Yes, and the Spirit was guiding me to do different things. I had this warm feeling in my heart, and it was like my heart began to speak to me and guide me."

"That's it," Nicole shouted very loudly. The row of kids sitting in front of them turned around and stared. Nicole smiled, and they sighed and turned back. Then she pulled out her journal and wrote:

Experiment 4:

HOLY SPIRIT

Jesus said a special counselor would come in his name to help people. The counselor is called the Holy Spirit.

My friend Elisha asked God to send her the Holy Spirit.

God sent the Holy Spirit. She felt a warm feeling inside her heart, and the Spirit is teaching her and changing her.

ONLY GOD CAN DO THIS.

Nicole looked up, and Elisha's eyes were filled with tears. Happy tears.

That night, Elisha unrolled scroll number two. She sat for a few minutes until she felt the Holy Spirit helping her, and then she wrote 'The message is talking about God.' She pulled her ruler out of her pencil box, and around the word God she drew an equilateral triangle. On the left side of the triangle she wrote 'Father,' on the right side she wrote 'Son,' and on the bottom she wrote 'Holy Spirit.' It was three in one. Just like the river in her dream.

Then she rolled up the scroll and turned off the light. And for the first time, in a long time, she closed her eyes and had a good night's rest.

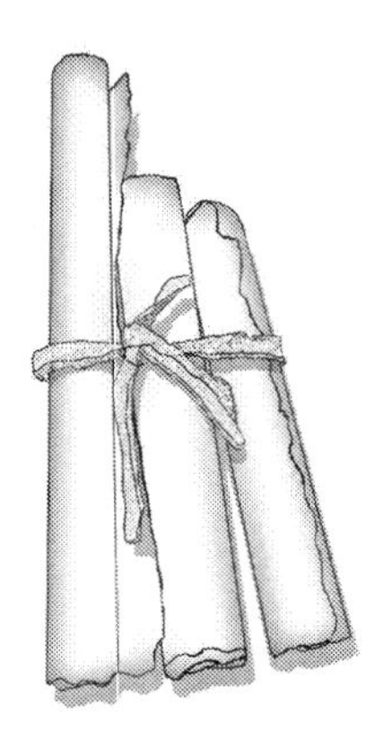

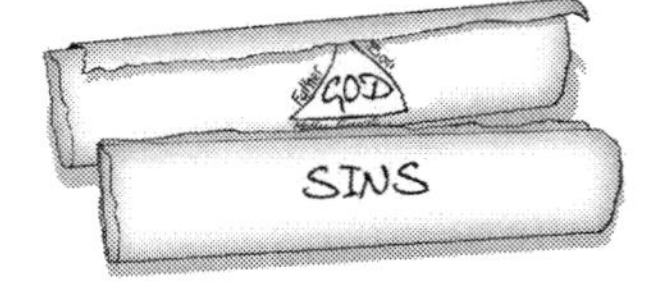

9

Talk to Me

Sitting next to the prayer box with a pencil in her hand, Elisha couldn't find the warm light in her heart, or hear the Holy Spirit's thoughts in her mind. And now that God was becoming her friend, she didn't like feeling this way. But most of all she didn't like wondering if she could go back to the kingdom.

She looked at the clock. 5:55 p.m. She closed her eyes and pictured the golden lamb. She remembered that if she stayed close she couldn't fall off. She remembered how she rode with her arms in the air. Have faith, she heard a small voice inside her say. Have faith.

And then she opened her eyes and wrote down, 'I pray to be even better friends with God.' She put the prayer into the box, and as soon as the paper touched the wood, she was standing in the kingdom with Angel Someone by her side. He was carrying a bucket of straw, and was dressed in his angel outfit.

"You made it. You made it," he said excitedly, putting down the bucket. "You must have completed the second scroll. Only three more scrolls left." He gave her a hug, and Elisha breathed in a strong smell of plastic.

"I can smell . . ." Then Elisha stopped speaking, worried it might be rude to say that he smelled like a troll.

"Plastic?" he asked. "It's okay," he continued. "People tell me I remind them of a troll because of the orange hair, and the . . ."

"Four fingers?"

Elisha and the angel started to laugh. Then Elisha moved her gaze away from Angel Someone, to the fields, and the rainbows, and the sky.

"Angel Gabriel's busy," he said. "He asked if I could come instead, and that you might want me to wear his angel outfit."

"There's just one little problem," Angel Someone said, looking down at the ground. "I don't have my flying license yet."

"You need a license?" Elisha asked, surprised that

God didn't give him all the powers he wanted. Angel Someone nodded. "Why can't you just take a test and get it?"

"Oh I have. I've taken the test 3,461 times," he said proudly.

"And you didn't pass?"

He smiled. "No, but I'm all signed up to take it again." Elisha didn't like taking a test twice, and once when she had to take a test three times, she had cried.

"Let's walk," he said, and he picked up the bucket and headed off to the edge of the field.

After a while they came to a large wooden gate. Elisha put her foot on the bottom rung, and started to climb over. "I've seen some thieves climb over gates like that," Angel Someone said. Elisha stepped down, she didn't want to be like a thief who had come to steal. Angel Someone stepped forward and swung the gate open so they could both walk through.

On the other side was a rather noisy flock of sheep. "Good morning," Angel Someone called, and the sheep recognized his voice and came running up to great him. They pushed closer and closer until they looked like one big curly body. There must have been a hundred of them. The wool tickled Elisha's legs and she stroked the top of one of the heads. Angel Someone stroked it too. "Hi Grace," he said.

Elisha leaned over to look closer at Grace. Her face was the same as all of the others; a black nose, curly brown hair, and two pointed ears that stuck out. "How do you know its name?" she asked.

"Well, I know each of them by name," Angel Someone said, patting another on its side. "I know my sheep, and the sheep know me." He smiled, then added, "But we'd better keep walking, I don't want their brother spending another night all by himself."

"You mean one of the sheep is all alone somewhere?" Elisha asked, hurrying behind Angel Someone as he scurried down a steep hill. The angel didn't answer, but instead was concentrating on walking down the slope which had now become very rocky. They held onto trees at the side so not to slip. They walked for a long time, away from the open pasture to an orchard at the bottom.

"Maybe the sheep's here," Angel Someone said, and he peered around the back of a large fig tree. But there

was nothing, only more fig trees lined up behind. So he peered around another tree, and another, and another. Angel Someone and Elisha looked behind tree after tree, traveling deeper into the orchard, until they arrived at the very center. And there, sitting on the ground all alone, was a sad looking, lost sheep. Angel Someone jumped up and down with excitement. "My lamb, we found my lost lamb!" he shouted joyfully. "It's a good thing to keep trying at something. This is such a happy day," and he gave him all the straw from the bucket, then carried him back to the pasture with the rest of the flock. He put the lamb down on the grass, but the lamb seemed shy about joining his brothers and sisters.

Angel Someone walked towards Elisha. “Now let me see that second scroll,” he said, looking at her bag as if he knew it was inside. She took the scroll out.

Angel Someone studied the triangle, the equal sides, and the word ‘God’ in the middle. “Father, Son, Holy Spirit,” he read, pointing to each of the sides. “You’ve done well. Do you also have the first scroll with you?”

Elisha handed it over, catching a glimpse of her long list of sins. Angel Someone read it and then said, “Jesus wants to have it.”

“What for?” Elisha asked, worried.

"He says he'll take care of it."

"Am I in trouble?" she asked, not understanding what he meant.

The angel's eyes became soft and he said, "Not at all. He knows you are sorry for all of the things on your list, and he is happy that you want him to be your best friend."

Elisha had never thought that she could make God happy.

"Oh yes," the angel said, in a confident voice. "He was happy when you walked in a new direction, and when you helped your sister at breakfast, and the children at recess. He was happy when you learned that Jesus was God."

"That was really Nicole who told me that," Elisha whispered.

"Yes, she's been helping you. But you chose to listen, you chose to follow the teachings of the Holy Spirit. And most importantly," Angel Someone said, "you chose to believe."

Then Angel Someone rolled up the scroll and said, "And now he has forgiven you for everything."

"All of it?" she asked.

"Yes," he replied, putting the scroll into the bucket where the straw used to be. "You don't need to carry it around anymore."

And Elisha's bag suddenly felt very light. No one had ever forgiven her for everything.

Angel Someone patted Elisha on the head as if she were one of the lambs. "I'll be back in a little while, but while I'm gone . . ."

"Seeds?" Elisha interrupted, knowing that it was about time for gardening.

"Only if you wouldn't mind." He handed her the familiar packet. On the outside was written ALMOST THE LAST OF THE FRUIT TREE SEEDS. Then he clapped his hands three times, and all the sheep's faces rose to look at him. "Now let's celebrate the return of your lost brother."

Elisha watched as Angel Someone guided the lost lamb back to its flock. He was such a tall angel, with big heavy hands, and wild orange hair that waved in the wind, like a flag showing the sheep which way to go. But he was also very gentle. He picked out spiky branches stuck in the sheep's thick wool. He wiped mud from their faces, and he sat for a while teaching them how to find water in the pasture.

But then Elisha became worried about time passing on earth, and she set off to plant her seeds. The field was green. The soil was rich and deep. No birds were in sight. Slowly she pushed each seed into the ground, covered them over, and patted the earth with her hands.

Elisha decided to stay and watch them grow. She would chase off birds and help water the roots. So she stayed at the end of the rows of seeds, and stared at the soil. Then she felt herself getting sleepy, and she stood up and walked around the garden. Around and around, watching for green leaves pushing through dark soil. But her legs became weary and her eyes were bored at looking at nothing. She sat back down and took a magazine out of her bag and began to read.

There was a story about a house built on the top of a mountain. It overlooked the city below and the owners had put real gold on all of the walls and on the edges of the doors. There was purple fabric flowing from the windows, rubies on the ceilings and at the bottom of the pool. A woman with strings of pearls was sitting outside the house, listening to musicians play for her. Elisha imagined herself living there, imagined herself sitting on the blocks of marble that covered the ground.

When the word 'ground' entered Elisha's mind, she remembered the seeds. But instead of putting her magazine down quickly, she continued to hold it in front of her face staring blankly at the pictures. She had the strongest feeling that it was already too late, that she had been reading too long, that the seeds had grown. A heaviness inside her also told her that something was wrong.

"You will need to look," Angel Someone said from behind her. "It is the only way to learn." He sat down next to her, and she slowly lowered the magazine.

In the patch of soil where the young trees should have been, were rows of thorny plants. They were thick, bristly, spiky. Elisha touched one and it poked her finger. Under the thistles, the young trees were bent over and choked. She tried to pull the thistle plants out, but the spikes dug into her fingers and they started to bleed. "I was sidetracked," she whispered, as if speaking to the withered seeds. "All those treasures in the house."

"Money sidetracks a lot of people," Angel Someone said, lifting her hands away from the soil, knowing that it was too late to help. "Money and worries about life gets people thinking about all the wrong things."

Angel Someone began to lead Elisha away from the garden, and back across the pasture to the sheep. "I wanted to give you some fruit," she said softly.

"One day you might," he grinned, and Elisha felt a small star of hope rising in her heart. Then the angel asked, "Elisha, when you felt the Holy Spirit did you feel the Spirit guiding you, talking to you?"

Her eyes lit up and she nodded. "Yes, like I knew what to do."

"To know all five secrets of this kingdom you must take great care of this Spirit.

Don't let the distractions of the world choke it out."

"Like the thorny plants choked out the young trees."

"Exactly," he said. Then his face became serious, and his eyebrows scrunched together like he was worried. "Be careful to remember what God teaches you. Be very, very careful."

"Is something bad going to happen?" she asked, thinking that he was trying to warn her.

He leaned in close. "Just be careful."

And then Angel Someone cupped his hands around his mouth and called to one of his lambs. The lamb came running towards him. Tucked under its collar was the third scroll. Elisha pulled the scroll out, and as soon as it was in her hand the light around her became brighter and brighter.

"One last thing," she called out to Angel Someone who was starting to disappear. "It's not that easy flying. Last time Angel Gabriel bumped his head on a tree." Elisha thought she heard him say "Maybe we can help each other," and then the light faded and she was standing in the clock tower.

The time on the clock was 6:05. Only ten minutes had passed since she had left. She sat down on the floor and unrolled the scroll. Written in the same writing as the other scrolls was a message:

On mountain tops and in valleys deep
I look for my lost and wandering sheep
My Spirit can see, my Spirit can hear
So talk to me lambs if you are near

Talking lambs. It was like Angel Someone's flock. Elisha had just begun to read the message a second time, when suddenly she heard a creaking on the stairs. Then it creaked again, louder. Someone was coming up the clock tower.

She hid the scroll in her bag and rushed to the staircase. She started to hurry down the steps, her feet going as fast as they could. Down the first six steps, and then down six more, and then she went around the corner, and there on the seventeenth step she stopped.

It seemed to Elisha that her breath and heart stopped too. She stood absolutely still. Right in front of her, like a long thin shadow created by the night, was the man with the black coat and hat.

10

Thistles

The man growled a deep sound like it was coming from the earth far below. Then he pushed his hat back so that Elisha could see his face clearly. His skin was pale, like he had never seen the sun, his eyes were staring at her with this angry piercing look.

"Time for that bird to go." He held up his pole, but now instead of a net on the end, there was a large wooden club. Elisha leaned away from him. He chuckled. "This time nothing's going to stop me." He swung the club above his head.

"No," Elisha screamed, and she heard the sound of the bird's wings flapping high above. The man heard it too and he looked up. Near the ceiling, behind one of the beams, they saw the edge of a white feather.

The man ran up the stairs and leaned towards the beam. "There it is," he laughed. Then he stopped and took aim.

"Fly," shouted Elisha. "Fly." But the bird stayed where it was. The man laughed loudly, held up his pole, and swung. The heavy wooden club came crashing down.

"Got it," he said. Then he pulled on his pole, but the end of his club was now stuck beside the beam, and it slipped from his hand. It swung back and forth above them. "Don't need it anyway," he said. "Bird's gone."

Elisha felt her heart flood with sadness, but before any tears could rise into her eyes, she caught a glimpse of a tiny beak moving behind the beam. Then she saw the end of a wing, and then the whole bird strut out. Perfectly healthy. Perfectly untouched. It even seemed to be smiling. It climbed onto the top of the club and swung back and forth, as if enjoying the ride.

"What?" questioned the man. "I missed?"

The bird cooed as if to say 'Yes,' then it fluttered to the light of the window.

The man stomped down the stairs and out of the tower. But Elisha knew that he would be back

"Thank you for staying," she whispered to the dove. "Without you here, they'd have closed the door."

It cooed again, and Elisha knew she had to hurry to solve the scroll. She pulled it out and read the third line, "My Spirit can see, my Spirit can hear." This scroll was going to be easy to solve. She had already learnt about the Holy Spirit, and how God even counted the number of hairs on her head. God could see. God could hear. The scroll was talking about God's Spirit being around her.

Elisha ran home excited. She was getting good at figuring out the messages. She didn't need the warning from Angel Someone about being careful.

At dinner her mind was all distracted thinking about the lost and wandering sheep. So when her dad asked if she wanted more pasta, she replied, "Talk to me lambs."

"What?" her mom asked, her eyes all wide with surprise.

"If you are near," she continued, finishing the line.

Her dad dropped the pasta spoon and it landed back in the bowl. It clanged loudly, and she suddenly realized what she had said. But it was already too late, her parents were peering over her with confused looking faces.

"Are you okay?" her mom asked, touching her forehead to check for a fever.

Her dad peered into her left ear. "Can you hear me?" he yelled.

"OW, dad. My ears are fine."

"Sorry," he said, and Elisha gave a heavy sigh. "It's just that we're worried," he continued. "Mom told me you disappeared for over an hour at church, and you seem so busy."

Elisha wanted to talk to her parents about all that was happening, but she didn't know how. Her mom came closer. "You're not in trouble are you?" she asked. "We want to help you if we can."

"But you need to tell us what's going on," her dad added, patting her on the head.

It was only two soft pats of his hand. Friendly and comforting like he had done hundreds of times before. But these were enough for Elisha to remember Angel Someone patting the sheep, and Angel Someone patting her. And the words on the scroll rose up into her mind:

On mountain tops and in valleys deep
I look for my lost and wandering sheep
My Spirit can see, my Spirit can hear
So talk to me lambs if you are near

And in one great moment, that was probably less than half a second, Elisha realized that she was one of the lambs too. God wanted her to talk to him. That was the lesson of scroll number three. Talk to God.

"You just helped," she laughed.

"We did?" her parents replied together.

"God wants me to talk to him."

"That's what you've been worried about?" her mom asked.

Elisha nodded. "Well," her dad said, "being worried about that is a good sort of trouble to be in. But if you need any help with it . . ."

Elisha thought for a moment and then asked, "A ride

to church tomorrow, and maybe some more pasta?" And her dad picked up the spoon and served some more.

That night in bed, Elisha unrolled the scroll, took out her pencil and wrote 'Talk to God' at the bottom of the page. She then rolled it up and put it back in her bag. She and God would soon be really good friends.

But the peace and the good night's sleep that usually came after solving a scroll did not arrive. Instead, she turned onto her right side, then she turned onto her left, she sat up and laid down, sat up again, laid down again. And when she still couldn't sleep she turned the light back on and looked at the scroll. On the bottom of the page was her writing, 'Talk to God.'

Talk to God. She had written the answer down, but she wasn't doing it. She wasn't talking to God. God didn't want her to just solve the message, but to actually do it.

She put the scroll away, knelt down on the floor, closed her eyes and said out loud, "Dear God, my name is Elisha." She stopped. It sounded more like she was writing a letter, and of course God already knew who she was.

She went back into bed, closed her eyes, and tried again. "Hey God, what's up?" She opened her eyes. Now it sounded like she was trying to be cool.

Then she had a really great idea. She found her sister's plastic cell phone. She could always talk on the phone. She opened it up, "Hi God, I wanted to talk to you about . . ."

But then the phone replied, "You have messages. Press five."

Elisha closed it up. One thing was clear. She didn't have any idea how to talk to God.

"Ready?" her mom asked the next morning, car keys in her hand. Elisha got up slowly from her chair. "You did want a ride to church?"

She didn't think she could take the scroll back before actually talking to God, but she said "yes" anyway, and climbed in the car.

Nicole was already at the church. She was on the stage with the rest of the dance team, practicing for a Sunday show. Pastor John and pastor Gilbear were playing the piano together. Elisha sat down to watch, amazed at how Nicole could bend over backwards making a perfect arch, how she could twist and turn, how the music seemed to lift her high off the ground, and she could land with a tiny bump. Nicole could dance and dance, and still have a big smile on her face.

In the break Elisha went up to her and whispered, "I have another question. How do you talk to God?"

Nicole wiped the sweat away with the back of her hand, took a sip of water and said, "Well you may think this is weird." Then she stopped talking.

"I promise I won't," Elisha replied.

Nicole looked around to see if anyone was listening, then she said, "Did you ever notice, before I start to dance I close my eyes for a few seconds?"

"Like you're scared or something?"

"No, not scared. I'm telling God the dance is for him, kind of a present. Then when I start to dance he's right there, listening and watching. And I think he can understand it all."

Elisha looked down at her own feet that seemed to

trip up from just walking along. "But what if you couldn't dance? How would you talk to him then?" she asked.

Nicole hesitated, "I don't know. I've always danced." And then pastor Gilbear started playing again, and Nicole skipped back to the stage.

Elisha left the hall. Talking to God shouldn't be that hard. If Nicole had found a way, she could too.

If she concentrated really hard she could talk to God. She walked along the path in the garden. "Your plants are growing," she whispered, "and your birds sound nice." Then she didn't know what to say, and she walked some more in silence. She just needed to practice.

She sat down at the entrance of the clock tower. "Talk to me," she thought. "Talk to me lambs if you are near." And then she began to feel something opening in her heart, like a door opens to the light, or a flower to the sun. It felt warm and welcoming, and words that she wanted to say to God started to flow into her mind. And she was just about to start speaking, when she heard the sound of a man laughing.

It was coming from the clock tower. It was the sound of the man with the black coat and hat. She ran inside.

He was bounding up the stairs to the top of the tower, leaping over three steps at a time, his heavy coat flying behind him. "Hey," Elisha shouted, but the man didn't even turn around. He had an idea. He was on his way to kill the bird.

Elisha went after him. She tried to skip a step, but they were too wide. She heard the thump, thump, thump, of his feet. He was nearly at the top. She was still at the bottom.

She ran as fast as she could. Up and up. And when she got to the top, he was standing in front of the clock, his arms stretched up high like the branches of a frozen tree in winter, his coat hung down blocking the light, so that the room was darkened. It took a moment for her eyes to adjust to the dim, but when they did her gaze drifted to his left hand. He was holding the wooden prayer box.

"The box," she shouted. Then her right hand moved up and covered her mouth, as if it was trying to keep these words inside her. But it was already too late, they had come out, and he knew the box was precious to her.

"The box," he repeated, "and the bird." He looked

up at the dove above them. He brought his arm back and took aim. Then he threw the box directly at the bird's right wing.

It hit the bird hard. Feathers flew into the air and the bird landed on its side. The prayer box fell, down, down the tower, and she heard it crash on the ground below.

Elisha looked up, and she saw through the beams that the bird was no longer moving. The man leaned towards her, close. "That's the end of your feathered friend," he hissed. Then he wrapped his coat around himself, and stomped back down the stairs, laughing.

Elisha stared at the dove, she watched the feet and the feathers, and the top of the small white head. She waited for the longest time, searching for the smallest sign of breath. But it did not move. This beautiful bird, that had stayed just to help her, was gone. How could she have let this happen? She should have know the man would be back. "I'm sorry," she whispered, but then she stopped speaking. Her words just sounded small and empty.

She dropped her gaze to the ground, turned her back to the clock, and slowly walked down the stairs, her shoulders hunched over like someone who had fought a great battle but had lost. She arrived at the bottom of the steps and saw the prayer box broken into hundreds of pieces. She almost bent down to pick a piece up, a souvenir to keep, but even this tiny movement was too much effort, and her arms and hands just hung by her sides as if drained of all energy. So instead, she shuffled out of the tower, leaving the bird and the kingdom behind her.

She walked onto the path that she had walked long before, and she remembered how lost she had felt, how she couldn't find her way. She shivered. The sun was out, but she felt dark inside. She felt cold. She felt like the lost lamb sitting in the center of the orchard, too many trees to find a way out.

"That man," she shouted, suddenly angry. She felt hate rising into her face, into her arms and hands. She made a fist. "That man," she shouted again, and she began to stomp her way along the path. She kicked a rock and it landed in the grass. Everything had gone wrong. It was all his fault.

And then she heard it again, his laugh. At first she thought she had imagined the sound, but when she turned she saw him sitting on a wall far from the church buildings. He was looking up at the sky. Then he turned, looked at her, and smiled. She walked towards him. Closer and closer until she was standing in his shadow.

Tears began to run down her face. The wind blew stronger and she closed her jacket and pulled her hands up into her sleeves. Then the man's shadow seemed to spread out over the land, making everything around her dark, and she looked up at the sky and saw that a large gray cloud had swallowed the sun. She thought of how she felt before she had gone to the Kingdom of Nain, before she had started to be best friends with God.

"Remember," she heard a small voice inside her

heart say. Was it the voice of the Holy Spirit? What did she need to remember? She tried to think, but couldn't.

The man's smile grew larger and he chuckled. "We can be friends," he said, holding out his hand, looking deep into her eyes.

She felt herself moving closer. What did she need to remember? His gaze was strong, like he was trying to draw her near. But just for a second she pulled her eyes away and she looked down, and there in the grass she saw a small plant. It was thick and spiky with prickly leaves. It was just like the thistles that had grown up among the fruit trees. It was choking out the flowers around it.

And she remembered. She remembered what Angel Someone had said. Be very, very careful. Be careful to think about God's teachings. Be careful of distractions.

She looked back up, Spirit rising in her now, a strength. The man's laugh stopped as if he knew. His smile turned to a frown.

And she felt the Holy Spirit tell her that this had been his plan all along. He hadn't wanted to get the bird out of the tower. It had been her, Elisha, that he had wanted. He had wanted to stop her from becoming best friends with God. She had been distracted with hating him, and had stopped thinking about the teachings of the kingdom.

Elisha stared at the man directly now. The Holy Spirit was with her. She was not afraid.

"My friend is God," she said firmly. The man lowered his hand, and as he did the sun burst out from behind the cloud, and his shadow pulled back to a small circle around his feet. His strength had shriveled in the light.

Elisha turned away and ran back to the tower, back up the stairs, and to the place where the bird lay. She knelt down. And she began to talk to God.

"Thank you," she said. "Thank you for wanting to be my best friend, and I'm sorry I forget sometimes. And thank you for my mom, and my dad, and my sister." Then Elisha was silent and even though her eyes were closed they couldn't keep her tears in.

"God, the bird. Can you help it?" Her voice became shaky, "It helped me, and can you help it? Please God, can you make it better?"

She was silent again for a moment, and then she remembered how pastor John always finished his prayers and she added, "Amen."

Elisha stayed kneeling on the floor with her eyes closed, and she felt like God was telling her not to worry, like God was telling her to trust Him. She imagined herself holding his hand, walking by his side. It was peaceful, like the sound of a dove cooing. The sound of a gentle dove's cooing.

She opened her eyes and looked up. There, above her, feathers a little messy, but clearly standing upright, was the bird. "Thank you," she shouted excitedly to God. "Thank you. Thank you," she said again, jumping up and down. God was great at miracles.

She raised her hands and the dove swooped down and circled around her head. Then it made a loud fluttering with its wings, and Elisha played chase with it around the tower, up and down the stairs, and when she got almost close enough to touch a feather, it winked and flew faster. Then they sat for a while, quietly in the light of the window, and Elisha began to realize something very important. The man could not stop her from being best friends with God. The distraction could not stop her. A broken prayer box could not . . .

She caught sight of the hundreds of pieces of wood on the floor. Could a broken prayer box stop her? Could it stop her from going back to the kingdom? She pulled out the scroll. The answer to the message was to talk to God. She knew how to talk to him, and she could practice anytime like walking in the garden or kneeling down in prayer. But did she need the box to return to the kingdom?

Elisha sat down next to the wooden pieces, and without really thinking about what she was doing, she began to play with them. She moved them around like pieces of a puzzle, sliding them left and right, up and down, putting them together into a shape on the floor. She stood up and looked at what she had made.

No, she didn't need a prayer box. The Holy Spirit was with her, inside her. She could pray to God at any time, talk to him whenever she wanted. She looked down at the shape made from all the broken pieces, and there on the floor was a perfectly formed, large, heart.

She held the scroll up to her own heart. It was all she needed to pray to God. She felt its beating under her hand, felt the Holy Spirit within.

"Will you teach me more God? Will you?" And the light around her became bright.

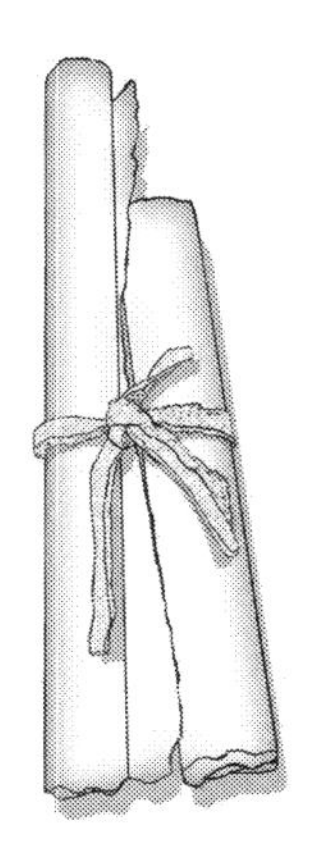

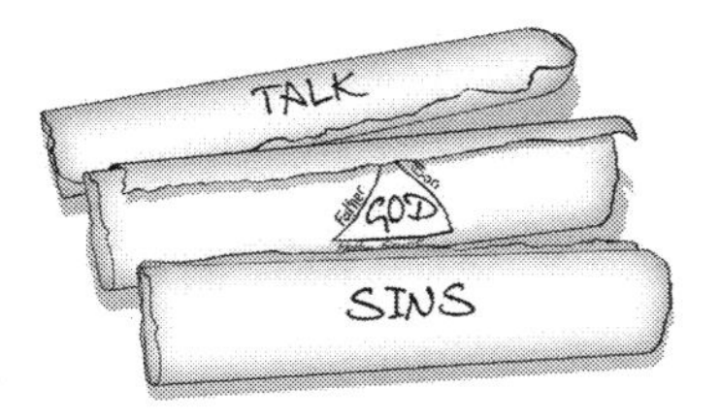

11

The Lamp

"That was close," said Angel Gabriel. "Did you doubt that you could come back?"

"Distractions, distractions, distractions," mumbled Angel Someone.

Both of the angels had come to greet her this time. They were standing next to each other. The tall, troll like figure, and Angel Gabriel in his robe and wings. A familiar looking sheep was at their side.

"Our lost lamb," said Angel Someone, stroking the top of his woolly head. "He's always wandering away." Elisha bent down to pet the lamb and it licked her forehead. It felt good to be back in the kingdom. The sun was beginning to rise, and the pure bright light touched the edges of the rainbows, floating like clouds across the horizon.

"The rainbows are moving," Elisha said excitedly.

"God must be using them," Angel Gabriel replied. "Why, sometimes he'll send out three hundred in one day." Angel Gabriel raised his trumpet to the skies and began to play, and the colors seemed to dance to his tune.

Angel Someone turned towards Elisha. "You must pick your field," he said, and she knew that he was talking about the fruit trees.

She saw the path where she had first scattered the seeds, and thought about the birds that had eaten them up. She saw the rock with the rich, dark soil that wasn't deep enough. No room for the roots to grow. She continued towards the field that looked so perfect, but was full of thistles waiting to choke.

Perhaps she now knew what was needed to make her fruit trees grow. Elisha walked on, feeling some excitement filling her heart. She looked up at the sky, and even though the sun had started to rise, there was a small bright star shining just above. Elisha stopped. This is where she would plant the next seeds.

Angel Gabriel handed her the familiar packet. On the outside was written THE LAST OF THE FRUIT TREE SEEDS.

"Come to the flock when you've finished," he said. "We'll be waiting for you there."

Elisha opened the packet and shook the round seeds into the palm of her hand. Then one by one she planted them, pushing them deep into the earth, covering them carefully with the soil. She stayed for a while to watch for birds, she stayed to watch for thistles. She kept her eyes on the soil, she kept her heart close to God by talking to him. She prayed that he would forgive her for any mistakes she had made, and asked that he help her not to make any new ones. She sat in the crystal light of the kingdom, feeling the warmth of the Holy Spirit. She thanked him for her family, and her friends, and the dove. "Please keep the bird safe," she prayed. "Keep it safe from the man in the black coat and hat."

Then, when her heart told her that it was time to leave, she got up and went to find the angels. She walked back along the path towards the flock. The sun had risen all the way now, but there were so many rainbows lined up on the path that every time she took a step, the ground seemed to change color. First she was walking on red, then yellow, then blue, and then she was back on red again and she thought she might have walked in a circle. She tried to listen for the sound of the sheep, as she knew they were not very far away, but all she could hear was Angel Gabriel speaking, and his voice seemed to come from all directions.

"Lost again?" It was Angel Someone, and he was standing right beside her. Elisha looked down at the ground, embarrassed.

"Of course you're still getting lost," he said. "You don't have everything you need yet." He held up a lantern and turned it on.

"A lamp?" Elisha asked.

Angel Someone smiled. He lowered the lamp to the path and the light shone onto their feet. "Hold this in front of you," he said. Elisha took the lantern, and held it out in front. The light shone onto the path, and she suddenly saw very clearly where the path went and where it did not.

"Thank you," she said, happy that she no longer had to guess which way to go. The sound of Angel Gabriel's voice became louder, and the woolly bodies of the sheep appeared.

Angel Gabriel was sitting in the center of the flock. On his lap was a large green book with post-its on the pages. He was reading the sheep a story. It must have been a good one, because when he saw Elisha and put the book away, the sheep made a soft, sad crying sound. "I see you've planted them all," Angel Gabriel said, taking the empty seed packet from her.

"Do you have the third scroll?" he asked.

Elisha sat down and took the scroll out of her bag. Angel Gabriel studied it carefully. "God was so happy when you talked to him."

"He was?"

"Oh yes, we all celebrated when we heard the news. You can't be best friends with someone if you don't talk to them." Elisha hadn't thought about this. It seemed so obvious now. She couldn't be best friends with someone at school if she didn't speak to them. It was just the same with God.

And then Angel Gabriel pulled out a long brown scroll from underneath his wings. "This is scroll number four," he said.

Elisha leaned forward excitedly, and was just about

to take it when she remembered the seeds. "I didn't check them," she said. "I should go back and make sure they're growing."

"That's good you remembered," said the angel, smiling. "But first you must complete the scroll. There is something very important that you don't have yet."

"What?" Elisha asked, her curiosity growing.

"Something special that will help you find your way, and keep you from going in the wrong direction."

"A lamp?' Elisha asked. "Like the one Angel Someone has?" She looked over at Angel Someone. His lamp had a strong metal handle, a blue base, and a tall flame flickering behind a glass globe. There didn't seem to be anything very special about it.

"If you solve the forth scroll you will out find what it is," said Angel Gabriel. Then his eyes started to twinkle, and he added, "And you will also discover the answer to another mystery."

"Which one?" Elisha asked. Angel Gabriel leaned closer and handed her the scroll. The light of the rainbows began to swirl together, and the angels, and the kingdom, disappeared.

12

A Mystery Solved

Elisha sat in the doorway of the clock tower with the scroll in her lap. A light rain mixed with the afternoon sun, and just a little way in front of her, stretching over the grounds, were two of God's rainbows.

"I knew you'd send one," she said. "But I never guessed two," and then the sun became stronger and the colors brighter.

Two rainbows. Two mysteries to solve. She stood up and walked towards the church hall.

Her mom and pastor Gilbear were setting up the chairs for the performance, and before even saying "Hello" or "How are you?" Elisha called out, "I know how to talk to God."

They both looked up from behind their rows. "How?" they asked together.

Elisha came over and said excitedly, "Well I've been practicing sharing what's in my heart, and telling him thank you, and asking for help with other things too."

They looked at her kindly. "That must make God happy," the pastor said smiling.

"That's weird, that's what Angel . . ." She stopped just before she was able to say "Gabriel said." The pastor's smile grew larger as if he knew something special, then he quickly turned to set up more chairs.

That night, Elisha unrolled the forth scroll. She ran her fingers across the paper, and she read:

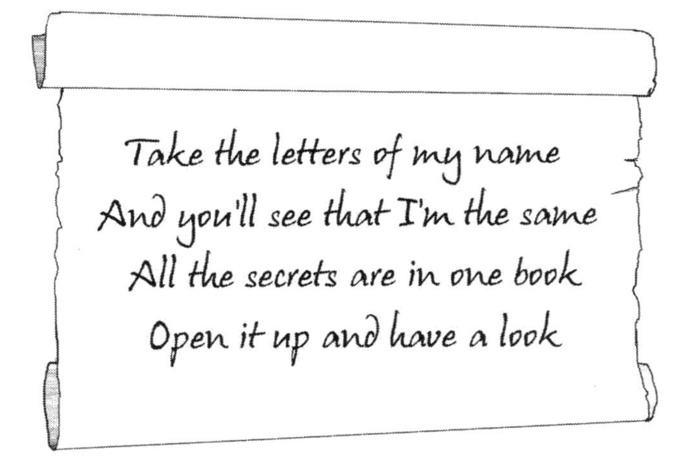

Elisha had no idea whose name the poem was talking about, or what the book was. It didn't matter though. Her faith was starting to grow like long, strong roots.

"I'll figure it out with your help God," she said.

And she turned off the light.

On Monday, she took the scroll to school and showed it to Nicole. “I don’t think pastor John’s talked about this,” Nicole said, tilting her head to the side, and staring at the paper with her tongue sticking out so the tip was showing. This was what she did when she didn’t know the answers to work in school, and Elisha knew that this time she would not be able to help. “Sorry,” Nicole eventually said, and handed it back.

“Don’t worry,” Elisha replied. “God will show me,” and she went off to the library to look for clues.

The library was full of books. Rows and rows of them. All the secrets are in one book. She pulled one off the shelf. It was a story about a girl and a pony. Quite a good story, but it didn’t say anything about secrets. “Will you show me God?” she prayed. She closed her eyes and reached up to grab another book.

“Elisha,” said a firm voice in front of her. She opened her eyes. It was Mrs. Winderland, the librarian. “Why are you pulling books off the shelf with your eyes closed?”

Elisha searched for something to say. “Well?” the

librarian said, louder now. Some of the other kids turned around to look. One of them was Mark. Muddy, soccer player, pants hanging down, Mark. Why couldn't she think of anything to say?

Mrs. Winderland moved her glasses lower down her nose, and peered over the top. The library became very silent, and Elisha wished that the recess bell would ring. And then, quite surprisingly, she remembered to talk to God. Her mind was all fuzzy from everyone looking at her, but from her heart she asked God what she should say.

And he told her to speak the truth. "I'm trying to solve a mystery," she replied.

Mrs. Winderland's face lit up. "I just love a good

mystery," and she led Elisha over to books about detectives, hidden treasures, and a dog that sniffed out lost school lunches. The other kids in the library started to talk again, and Mark walked over.

"I've read a lot of these," he said, leaning on the shelf. "Like this one's really good." He pointed to a cover with stolen dinosaur bones on the front.

Mark was trying to help. She had been so mean to him, and he was trying to be kind. She wanted to say that she was sorry about all the underpants tickets, that she hadn't been a good friend, that she had put it on her list of mistakes and was trying to change.

He shuffled his feet around nervously and asked, "So what mystery are you trying to solve?"

Elisha had the scroll with her, and her fingers started to tingle like she wanted to show it to him. Mark. Underpants Mark. Would God really send someone like Mark to help her? Then, before she could think about it anymore, she pulled it out and read him the message.

He was silent for what seemed like a very long time, then he said, "Once in this mystery book the clue was written down as an anagram."

Anagram. She had heard the word before but

couldn't remember what it was. "Anyway, I think that's what it's talking about."

"Anagram. Thanks," she smiled. And then the bell rang.

Her dictionary at home said that an anagram was a word made from the letters of another word. It gave an example. If you scrambled the letters of "weak," you could also make the word "wake."

Mark was smarter than she had thought. He had figured it out quickly. Now she just needed to find out whose name the message was talking about. "Thanks, God," she said, "for letting Mark help." And she felt her heart becoming warmer and stronger. She turned off the light and closed her eyes, and as she fell asleep she sensed a warmness around her.

"I'm not sure anything's in there," her mom said the next morning, as Angela shook out the cereal almost to the end.

Elisha took the box and peered inside. "I don't see anything either," she said. "But it'll come out soon. There's only a few bowls left."

Her sister's eyes went wide with fear. "What's the

matter?" Elisha questioned.

Her sister didn't speak, and then Elisha realized that Angela was afraid she was going to take the last bowls. Elisha put the box down. "Think I'll start eating toast in the mornings," she said, and her sister gave a happy little jump in her chair.

Sometimes it was more fun to be kind.

Elisha's school work that day was covered with names in the margins. As Mark had found the clue she put his name first. She wrote down the letters M, A, R, K. She saw the word "ark" but then didn't know what to do with the letter M. She continued on. "Principle" became "rip pencil." "Borris" became "Sir Rob." She put the words together and got "Sir Rob Rip Pencil," but didn't think this had anything to do with her being best friends with

God. And she was just writing down the letters of one of the after school staff, when her teacher, Ms. Judd, came over.

"This doesn't look like math," she said, staring at all the scribbles on the paper. Elisha remembered that she had forgotten to write down Ms. Judd's name.

"You need to finish sections one and two," Ms. Judd continued.

J, U, D, D, Elisha thought. Not great letters for making a word.

"Elisha," her teacher said firmly. Elisha looked up and her teacher took the scribbles away.

All that week during recess, lunch, gym, after school, and at home, Elisha continued to make anagrams in her head. Every time she spoke to someone, she started moving the letters of their name around in her mind. She became quite skilled, even turning "Nicole" into "no lice." There was nothing, however, about God.

On Sunday morning she read the scroll again. 'And you'll see that I'm the same.' Who was the same? Who was the scroll talking about?

She sat down and closed her eyes. "Thank you God

for teaching me more. I don't always get it right away, so please could you keep helping me, and could you help Angela find the surprise in the cereal box?"

There was a peaceful feeling in the room when she opened her eyes, and the letters and names that were jumping around in her head became still, like an ocean becoming smooth in the middle of a storm. The soft light of sunrise filtered through the window.

She felt happy that she had so much help. It would be hard to solve the scrolls all on her own without God, without the angels, without the pastors from the church. She remembered how pastor Gilbear had told her he had been sent to the church to help all those who wanted to be closer to God.

The angels. The pastors. She hadn't seen them all week, so had forgotten to write their names down. Her mind started to play with the letters of their names, but this time she was calm, focused. She took out her pencil. Their was Angel Someone and Gabriel, pastor John and Gilbear.

It was when she came to the last name that her writing slowed down. Carefully she made the G, and dotted the i. With concentration, she added the l, and the b, and the ea, and r. Her eyes saw it immediately. Her heart knew it was right. Take the letters of my name. G-I-L-B-E-A-R. And you'll see that I'm the same. G-A-B-R-I-E-L. Their names had the same letters.

Angel Gabriel was pastor Gilbear.

"No," she shouted jumping up and down excited. "No wonder," she said, remembering all the little things that had been bothering her.

That's how pastor Gilbear had known about her wanting God to be her best friend, and why Angel Gabriel had a bike that looked just like the pastor's. No wonder there were still bread pieces in the basket, and that Angel Gabriel and pastor Gilbear had that same look in their eyes.

It had seemed natural for Elisha to meet the angels in the Kingdom of Nain, but she never would have imagined that she would be visited by an angel on earth, in her very own church. It was a miracle that God would send an angel to watch over her, and deliver messages like sometimes a broken bicycle can be a part of his plan.

Nicole had once said that there were angels on the

earth that protected you wherever you went, that God could send one out to keep you safe. She thought about how pastor Gilbear was there the night she was so cold and lost on the dark path, and how he had handed her a loaf of warm bread and helped her to find the way.

He was God's angel on the earth to protect her.

And then, as if guided by something other than herself, her mind drifted to all the people she spoke to every week; the people at school, and church, and even out in the park. Were some of them doing the work of angels? Were some of them delivering God's messages? And she thought that she needed to remember to be kind to everyone, because one of these people might just be an angel in disguise.

Elisha picked up the scroll again and wrote, "Pastor Gilbear is Angel Gabriel."

Then she ran down the stairs. "Mom, can we go to church now? I have to find pastor Gilbear!"

13

Hear Me

"I'm sorry," pastor John said. "He already left."

"When's he coming back?" Elisha asked.

They were standing outside the church hall. Elisha had run all the way from the car. Her heart was beating double speed, her words were all choppy from lack of breath.

"I can wait," she added, jumping up on the wall. "It's very important."

Pastor John's eyebrows moved together in a worried look. "I'm really sorry," he said.

The way he pronounced the word "really" extra slow did not sound good to Elisha, but she was not at all prepared for what he said next. "Pastor Gilbear's left our church and gone home. He was only meant to stay for a little while."

"He's not coming back?" Elisha asked, stunned. "Ever?"

"No," said pastor John softly. "He already lengthened his stay by a couple of weeks. Something about needing to finish a project with a scroll."

"But it's not finished," Elisha shouted. "It's not finished!"

Pastor John looked confused. "I don't think pastor Gilbear would go away without completing his work. He wouldn't leave things half done."

Elisha suspected that this was true. But then why, she wondered, was the message talking about him? Why did the scroll mention his name if he wasn't going to guide her to the book? "He was helping me with something," she said, looking sadly at her bag with the scroll inside.

Pastor John sat down on the wall next to her. "We're all going to miss him."

"Are you sure he's not going to come back? Not even for a day?"

"No, not even for a day." Then he said, "But maybe I can help you."

Elisha didn't want to be rude, but she didn't think that pastor John could solve the mystery this time. Even Nicole had said that he had never talked about the message, and she listened to everything he said.

And then she remembered that help sometimes comes from unexpected places, like the way Mark had helped her in the library. She never would have thought that he could have solved the first part of the riddle. Well, maybe pastor John could solve the rest.

"I'm looking for a book," she said.

Pastor John jumped off the wall, as quickly as if his pants were on fire. His eyes widened and he threw his arms up in the air, like rockets shooting to the sky, and he shrieked "I forgot all about it!"

"What?" Elisha asked. But pastor John wasn't listening. He was leaping around all worried looking as if he was trying to put the fire out.

"Stop. Drop. And roll," Elisha shouted. Pastor John stopped. "That's what they teach us in school, and you're jumping around like you're on fire."

His whole body stilled, and the flame in his eyes turned to a smile. Then he bent down to her height and asked, "Will you forgive me?"

"For what?"

He hesitated for a moment, then said, "I promised

pastor Gilbear I wouldn't forget. He gave me a package for you. I think it might be a book. He said when you come looking for him, I'm to give it to you."

"He did?" she asked, jumping off the wall now too. Then she said, "And of course I forgive you."

"Are you sure?"

"Yes, I'm sure. But if you're worried about it tell Jesus. He takes care of people's mistakes." And pastor John's face beamed with happiness.

The package was wrapped in brown paper. It was heavy like a book, and her name was written on the outside. She took it to the clock tower, settled down in the doorway next to the bird, and then opened it up.

It was the large, green book that Angel Gabriel had been reading to the sheep on her last visit. She recognized the post-its marking the pages. She turned the cover, and inside she saw that pastor Gilbear had written her a note.

It said:

Dear Elisha,

In your hands is the number one best selling book of all times! Nobody has ever, or will ever write a book as popular as this one. (Although many people have tried).

This book is thousands of years old, but don't be worried about its age, because this is God's book. He told people what to write down. And He is the best author ever.

It is God's story, from the very beginning of time. It is like His own private journal, and He has given it to us to read.

Be careful of it though, because it is a miraculous book. It has great power. It will be a lamp to your feet, and a light to your path. It will guide you to new and wonderful places.

All the secrets you ever need to know are in this book.

Happy Reading,

Pastor Gilbear

Elisha turned to the next page and read the title of the book: The Bible.

Pastor John had talked about the Bible. He had read from it many times, but she had never really understood what it was. So this was God's story. His journal. She opened it up to one of the post-its. On the paper pastor Gilbear had written: This was written by one of Jesus' best friends. His best friends are called disciples.

Some of the page was underlined. Elisha read:

'At that time the disciples came to Jesus and asked, "Who is the greatest in the kingdom of heaven?"

He called a little child and had him stand among them. And he said: "I tell you the truth, unless you change and become like little children, you will never enter the kingdom of heaven.'

Elisha sat very still. Become like little children. Adults were always telling her to grow up and stop being like a child, but God was saying that there was something about children that he really, really liked. God was saying that the adults needed to be more like kids.

"Thank you," she said, looking up at the sky. "Thank you for putting that in your book." She couldn't wait to tell Nicole. She couldn't wait to read more.

She turned to another underlined section, where pastor Gilbear had written: Read this true story – Only God can do this.

She read:

'Soon afterward, Jesus went to a town called Nain, and his disciples and a large crowd went along with him. As he approached the town gate, a dead person was being carried out—the only son of his mother, and she was a widow. And a large crowd from the town was with her. When the Lord saw her, his heart went out to her and he said, "Don't cry."

Then he went up and touched the coffin, and those carrying it stood still. He said, "Young man, I say to you, get up!" The dead man sat up and began to talk, and Jesus gave him back to his mother.'

Elisha read the story a second time. The dead son was in a coffin ready to be buried, and Jesus just told him to get up, and he had come back alive, sat up, and talked! She looked at the white dove about her. "He made you better too," she whispered. And then she noticed that the town was called Nain. Just like the kingdom. Perhaps that was why pastor Gilbear had underlined it.

She ran her hands across the smooth paper. God's diary. In her hands. So God wasn't just a warm feeling in her heart, or someone to pray to. God could speak. And through the words in this book, he could speak to her. She could pick up the Bible at any time and be close. Just like reading a note from a friend.

Elisha remembered the thorns, the distractions, the things that kept her from being close to God. She remembered too what Angel Gabriel had said, that she didn't have everything she needed yet. That there was something missing to help her find her way.

She looked back at the book. God's words. This was the missing piece that would guide her. This was the answer to the forth scroll.

Elisha pulled out scroll number four, and next to the

poem she wrote, "God speaks. His words are written down in his book, the Bible." Then underneath she added, "God told me he really likes kids."

Elisha turned to the next page of the Bible to put the scroll inside, but just as she was closing the book, her eyes fell on another underlined section. In the margin was written, "Elisha, this is your story. Remember it well."

Her story. In the Bible. Could it be possible? She read :

'A farmer went out to sow his seed.'

"Seeds," she said out loud to the dove above. "I know all about seeds."

The dove fluttered in excitement, and for the first time it flew gently down next to her, just a few feet away from the entrance of the clock tower door. Then it stood very still, staring right at her with an "I want to hear the story" look.

"Well, if Angel Gabriel can read to the sheep, I guess I can read to you," she said. The bird sat down as if ready to listen.

Elisha started the story again, reading out loud. "A farmer went out to sow his seed. As he was scattering the seed, some fell along the path; it was trampled on, and the birds of the air ate it up."

The dove stood up suddenly, and began to move quickly towards the doorway. "Come back. You're not in trouble," Elisha said. "The story's not talking about you."

The bird kept going, fluttering its wings as if it was about to fly away. "You didn't eat the seeds," Elisha called out louder this time. But the bird took another step closer to the door. "I'll keep reading," she said. "Maybe if I get past the bird bit."

Elisha continued, "Some fell on rock, and when it came up, the plants withered because they had no moisture."

She stopped and looked at the dove. Now it was at the very entrance of the door. One more step and it would be outside. She continued to read, "Other seed fell among thorns, which grew up with it and choked the plants."

The dove turned its head towards her, its eyes gentle and full of love. And Elisha realized that the dove wasn't leaving because it was angry. The dove was leaving because it was happy. It knew that she no longer needed it. Her new guide, the Bible, was now in her hands.

"Thank you," she said, happy tears now falling from her eyes. "Thank you for risking your life for me." The bird cooed a long joyful sound. Then it raised its wings and began to fly. Up, up, and out of the clock tower.

And as it began to fly Elisha read, "Still other seed fell on good soil. It came up and . . ."

The bird disappeared into the sky, and Elisha, before she could finish the story, found herself sitting in a field in the Kingdom of Nain.

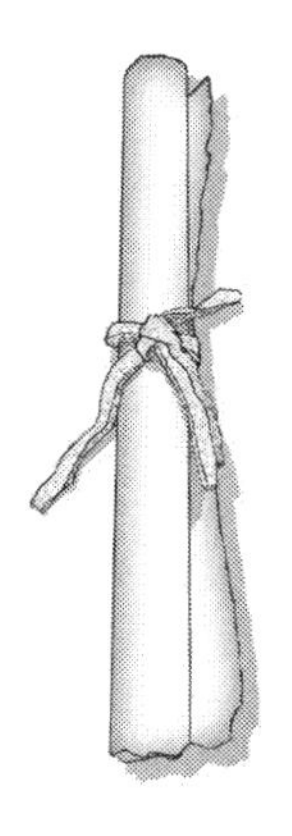

14

For One of God s Angels

"And what do you think happened then?" Angel Gabriel asked the sheep. They started to talk amongst themselves as if they couldn't decide.

"Angel Gabriel," Elisha shouted, jumping up excitedly. The Bible slipped from her lap. She caught it, but the scroll fell out and she lost her place. "Or maybe I should call you pastor Gilbear?" she said, handing over the scroll.

Angel Gabriel looked down at the scroll and read in a rather shy voice, "Pastor Gilbear is Angel Gabriel." He pointed to the bottom of the page and his voice became louder, "God speaks. His words are written down in his book, the Bible. God told me he really likes kids."

"Good job Elisha. You solved the forth scroll. It's so important to listen to what God has to say. The other person is having so much trouble.

"The other person?" Elisha questioned. "Who's the other person?" The angel suddenly looked worried as if he had said too much. "Do I know them?" she asked.

The angel didn't reply.

"Maybe Jesus can help," she suggested.

Angel Gabriel's eyes became sad, and he shook his head slowly. "Jesus wants to help, he really does. He's been walking next to this person all their life. Waiting."

"Waiting for what?"

"For the person to open their heart and let him in. That's all it takes," he said excitedly. "We've had all sorts of people do it. It's as simple as opening a door. Jesus is standing just on the other side."

"Then why don't they do it?" Elisha asked. "Why don't they just open the door?"

The angel shook his head sadly, and then got up and went over to the sheep and began to care for them, giving them straw to eat. He sat down next to the one who had been lost, stroking his head. He had a look in his eyes like he was grateful he had been found, but he knew there were more out there somewhere.

Then after a few minutes he came back to Elisha and said, "You only have one scroll left."

"And I have the Bible to guide me now," Elisha replied. "It has all God's stories and it has mine too." She started to turn the pages looking for the story of the seeds. "If I can just find the place," she mumbled, looking at all the underlined sections.

"Would you like us to go find it?" Angel Gabriel asked.

"Where?" she said, not understanding what he meant.

He pointed towards the rainbows and fields. Elisha looked at the rainbows lined up on the path, and she remembered it was where she had planted the last of the fruit tree seeds. She hesitated. They were the last of the seeds.

So instead of answering right away she said, "There were some clues you forgot to hide when you were disguised as pastor Gilbear."

Angel Gabriel turned to face Elisha. His eyes were so bright, so full of love, that she could hardly look at them. "Like the pieces of bread in the basket?" he asked.

"You put them there on purpose?"

"Just a few crumbs to help you find your way," he laughed.

Elisha had a lot of help to find her way. It seemed she was always getting lost. And now that she knew which direction to go, she was afraid. Afraid to step onto the path. One of the sheep came running up. It nibbled at her feet and nudged her legs with its nose.

"Grace wants to see if the fruit trees have grown," Angel Gabriel said. "I started reading them the story the other day, but just didn't have time to finish it."

Grace gave a long baa, and Elisha looked down at the sheep's face. Her big brown eyes pleaded with her, and she remembered how Angel Gabriel's letter had said that the Bible would take her to new places. "Let's go," she said suddenly, and all the sheep started running around excitedly. Then they lined up on the path.

"Are they all coming?"

"Oh yes," said Angel Gabriel. "All of the sheep want to see what happened to the last of the fruit tree seeds."

They began walking towards the field, stepping through the rainbows. They walked closer and closer, moving quickly over the rocks along the path. The sheep's noses started to twitch in the air as if they smelled the trees, and their ears stuck up straight as if listening for the sound of them growing. Elisha wasn't confident about walking fast, or about stepping through the very last rainbow before the field.

"Are you sure you want to look?" Angel Gabriel asked.

Elisha wasn't sure. She wasn't sure at all, but then she remembered and said, "It is the only way to learn." Her eyes were actually closed when she said this, and she thought about all the things that had gone wrong before. The birds. The shallow soil. The thorns.

So when she started to open her eyes, her thoughts

were on how the seeds would not have grown, how the plants would be small and withered, how the field would be bare. And when her eyes were fully opened, it took a few seconds for her mind to realize what she was looking at.

In front of her stood hundreds of trees. They were tall, strong trees, and their branches which stretched out above her were covered in leaves and fruit like she had never seen before. They had grown. They had all grown. Every single one of the seeds was now a magnificent tree.

The sheep gave several jumps in the air. Angel Gabriel waved his arm towards the trees, "Go look, go look," he said, and they scurried off into the orchard.

For a moment Elisha had a doubt and she asked, "These are from the seeds I planted?" Angel Gabriel smiled warmly, and she knew they were from the very same seeds.

She stepped towards one of the trees. It had long blue fruit shaped like drops of water. The wind blew, and the fruit moved and rippled like waves on the ocean. And it was only when she touched one of the fruit, that she realized they were solid.

She sat down underneath the tree. "Did the fruit trees grow because of what I did?" she asked Angel Gabriel. "Because of things like helping my sister and not giving Mark tickets?"

"Come," said Angel Gabriel, and they walked deeper into the orchard, past a tree with red fruit the shape of hearts. Angel Gabriel picked one of them.

"The trees would have grown even if you hadn't done those things," he said.

"Then why did they grow this time?" she asked.

He put the fruit into the palm of her hand. It was soft, sweet smelling. "You welcomed God into your heart. You believe in him. You trust in him. That is why the seeds have grown."

He leaned against a trunk. "The trunk is like the faith you have in Jesus. It is solid, with long, strong roots." He picked a fruit, a deep yellow one, shaped like the letter 't'. "The fruit is what has grown because of your faith."

Elisha knew that God was becoming her best friend, and that many good things were growing because of it.

Then Angel Gabriel clapped his hands twice and the

sheep came running to him with baskets in their mouths, and a basket even miraculously appeared next to Elisha's feet. She placed her Bible inside. "Now everyone," he said joyfully. "Let's begin the harvest."

He turned to Elisha, "Could you pick from the tree with the deep yellow fruit?" he asked. "I will pick from the tree with the red." Then he called to the flock, "And you are free to wander where you wish." Then Elisha and Angel Gabriel filled their baskets with the fruits of the kingdom.

"Wonderful," said Angel Gabriel to Elisha. "You will have fruit to give to Angel Someone."

And the fruit that Elisha picked for him smelled sweet and rich. First fruits from the new trees, for one of God's angels.

15

Four Fingers

With only four fingers, Angel Someone chose to hold the "t" shaped fruit upside down. "Do you need help?" Elisha asked.

Angel Someone looked up, the juice of the fruit dripping as he took a bite. "No need," he said. "This is the best way for a troll like me to eat this fruit." And then, as if suddenly realizing what he had revealed, he stayed very, very, still.

Angel Someone stared at Elisha. Elisha stared at Angel Someone. A silence grew between them until Elisha shouted, "So you are a troll! The plastic. The four fingers. The big smile and hair." Then, before she could think about what she was saying, she blurted out, "Aren't trolls supposed to be mean?"

He looked at her gently. "And how can a troll be an angel in the kingdom?" he said, finishing the question.

Elisha felt bad, it wasn't a nice thing to ask, but it was what she was wondering.

Angel Someone wiped his sticky fingers on the grass. Then in a soft, calm voice, he said, "I was born on the earth about five years before Jesus."

Angel Someone was old. Really old. The wind suddenly strengthened, and his orange hair blew wildly around his face and up above his head. His smile faded and his expression became serious, and he said, "I did some terrible things," and Elisha believed this to be true because he suddenly looked very much like a wild troll. And in his eyes, deep in his eyes, she thought she saw something that she hadn't seen before. It was like looking into a lake and thinking that you see a shadow far below the surface, but not being sure what it was.

"I would like to know," Elisha said, her voice strong, like she desperately needed to know.

"Then I'll tell you," he replied. Elisha moved closer. She wanted to say that she had made mistakes too, but he probably already knew this. So she stayed silent, and she heard the sound of the wind, and saw some of the rainbows fading.

"I had made my home under the darkest bridge in the woods," he said. "I stayed there alone, day and night, sitting underneath, listening for the sounds of the animals crossing.

"I was hungry, and I believed that I was the greatest troll there was, that I knew everything. Then one day, three goats came, and I thought I was going to kill one to eat. But they tricked me, they laughed at me, they threw me in the water. They told the rest of the goats what had happened, and they mocked me too." Angel Someone paused, then he said, "Anger entered my heart."

Angel Someone glanced up at Elisha, checking that she wanted him to continue. She nodded, and he said, "A few months later, I saw something I had never seen before. A new kind of animal came over the bridge, a new type of sheep. They were different from the rest. They said they had found a pasture where the water flowed freely, and with just one sip, they were never thirsty again. They said the water could bring you peace. They said the water could make you kind. I didn't believe them, and I was filled with even greater anger, and I became even meaner. And I hated them for being so full of joy. I hated them more than I had hated any other animal before."

He paused, and the wind whipped his long hair across his face, as if trying to keep hidden what he was going to say next. He pushed it back, and in a low voice he said, "So I came out from under my bridge, and I went to hunt these new sheep. I hurt them. I killed them. I had them taken from their flock. I was a very mean, and powerful, and ugly troll."

Elisha couldn't imagine this. She couldn't imagine him doing these things. Not Angel Someone. Tears arose in her eyes.

"It's true," he said, and he reached out and held her hand, and it didn't feel mean at all. He felt warm, and gentle, and loving.

"What happened?" she asked

"These new sheep started to appear all over the place. Hundreds were saying that they had found the pasture and drunk the water. I heard that some were in a town nearby, so I went on a journey to find them.

"It was just after Jesus had died. I knew he was dead because a friend of mine had seen him buried. The new sheep were saying that Jesus was God. I thought they were telling lies, making up more stories. I thought Jesus was just an ordinary man."

Angel Someone's eyes grew soft, the wild look was gone. Angel Someone looked at Elisha, and the shadow in his eyes grew strong, and she realized that it was sadness. A deep, deep, sadness far below.

"A flash of light," he said. "This bright light flashed down from heaven while I was walking along the road, and a voice like God thundered down to me, 'Troll, troll, why are you killing my sheep?'

'Who are you Master?' I asked.

'I am Jesus, the one you are hurting. Now get up and go into the city, and you will be told what you must do.'

"When I got up I couldn't see. I was blind, and for three days I couldn't eat or drink. I had never felt so sick, so sad. I had been wrong. The sheep were right. Jesus was God. And every time I hurt the sheep, I was also hurting God."

"What did you do?" Elisha asked, thinking how impossible it would be to make things right again.

"I didn't do anything," Angel Someone said. "It was

God. God sent one of his friends to help me. He put his hands over my eyes, and these things like scales fell from my eyelids. And I could see.

"I could see my feet and hands, and the sun rising outside the window. I could see Jesus' friend standing there, helping me, even though I had hurt the flock. I could see that Jesus was kind and loving, and that he had forgiven me for all the terrible, terrible things I had done, and I felt as though I had drunk from the waters of the pasture.

"I stood up, and I started to tell everyone, 'The sheep are right. The sheep are right. Don't hurt them. They are right.' And I wrote letters saying this, and I traveled from North to South, and East to West, speaking to as many as I could.

"And at first people replied, 'Aren't you that ugly old troll who told us the sheep were wrong?' or 'Aren't you that mean troll who wants to kill the new sheep?'

'I am he,' I said. 'But I was wrong, and the sheep are right. Jesus is God. Jesus is God and he can love you, just as he has loved me, no matter what you have done. All you need is faith.'"

Angel Someone picked up the basket of fruit that Elisha had picked. "The deep yellow fruit is the fruit of faith," he said.

He handed one to Elisha and she took a bite. It was sweet, and it quenched her thirst. It was as if all her favorite flavors had risen up from the earth into it.

Angel Someone smiled, and as he did, the fifth scroll appeared on top of her Bible. Elisha picked it up, and the kingdom and the angel started to disappear, but his voice remained strong. "This is why an ugly old troll can become an angel in the kingdom," he called. "Forgiveness and faith."

Then, as his voice was fading she heard him say, "The thing you need next will fall under the table."

16

Different Parts

Elisha couldn't believe that she was holding the last scroll. The very last scroll.

She unrolled it, expecting to find a poem about God, but instead she saw something rather strange:

Imagine your body as one big foot
What would you do if you wanted to look?
Imagine your body as a giant eye
How would you eat your favorite pie?

Elisha put the scroll down and did what the poem asked. She imagined herself as a huge foot. She pictured the heel, the toes, the nails, and she smiled at how

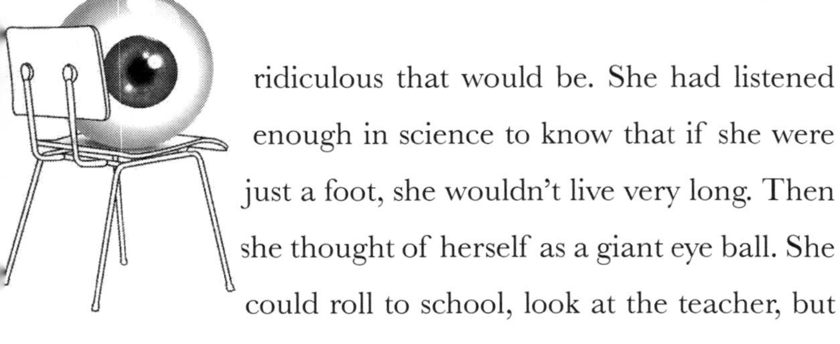

ridiculous that would be. She had listened enough in science to know that if she were just a foot, she wouldn't live very long. Then she thought of herself as a giant eye ball. She could roll to school, look at the teacher, but she certainly wouldn't be able to eat anything, let alone her favorite pie, which happened to be blackberry and apple.

"Okay God. I did what the poem asked," she said, confident that he would help. "Now can you show me what falls under the table?"

She got up and walked around the house. She went into her dad's office and stood by his desk, but the only thing on it was his computer and the wind wasn't even blowing.

"Oh no," her dad said from the doorway. "You have that look again, the one you always get when you need to answer a question."

"I'm waiting for something to fall under the table," she said.

Her dad's right eyebrow raised in disbelief. "Sure," he said, moving further away. He took a step backwards out of the room. "I'll be back later," and he disappeared around the corner.

That week, Elisha checked the tables in the cafeteria and the classroom. She opened up all the windows on a very blustery day. Papers blew off the tables, but not under them. A science experiment blew over, her work blew outside, and her teacher blew up. "Elisha," she shouted, "Close the windows." The whole class stared at her. Except for Nicole. She came over to help.

"I need to find something that falls under the table," Elisha whispered, as they tried to capture the ants that had now escaped from the experimental farm.

Nicole knew immediately that this had to do with the scrolls, and with God. So she whispered back, "You can't make God's plans happen. You have to be patient. You have to listen." Elisha thought about the fruit of faith. She picked up two ants and put them back safely. "You can trust him," Nicole said.

By Sunday, Elisha had stopped trying to make things fall, and she had stopped watching the tables for long periods of time. Instead, she just tried to be ready for when the moment came. She kept her Bible, her scroll, and her pencil in her bag.

On Sunday, the youth room was crowded. Pastor John was standing at the front, reading something from God's book. Elisha saw Nicole, and she sat down next to her. Pastor John turned the page and read, "As it is, there are many parts, but one body."

Parts. One body. Elisha stared at pastor John in shock. This was what the scroll had been talking about. Parts of the body. The foot. The eye.

Pastor John continued reading, "The eye cannot say to the hand, 'I don't need you!' And the head cannot say to the feet, 'I don't need you.'"

Elisha sat very still. Was the Holy Spirit helping her?

"What does this mean?" pastor John asked.

Before she even had time to think, Elisha put her hand up in the air. "Elisha," pastor John said, as if surprised.

"It means you can't just be something like a giant eyeball and roll around and go to school. I mean, how could an eyeball eat a pie?" Everyone, including Elisha, laughed.

"She's right," said pastor John. "That's exactly what it's about. A body isn't just made up of one piece, like a foot, or an eyeball." He looked at Elisha directly when he said "foot" and "eyeball," and she felt as if the Holy Spirit was speaking to her.

"A body is make up of many parts. Hands, feet, eyes, legs. They all have different but important jobs."

Pastor John closed the Bible, and he stretched his arms outward as if trying to hug the whole room of youth. He said, "We are like one body. The body of Jesus. Each of us has a different job."

One of the boys raised his hand and said, "I don't get it."

"You are like the mouth," said pastor John. "You ask questions so that we may all understand." The boy sat up proudly.

Another boy crumbled up a piece of rubbish and dunked it into the trash. Pastor John pointed to him. "You're the hands, keeping God's house clean."

"I'll be the feet," shouted a girl, jumping up and down.

"I'll be the body dancing," said Nicole, doing a leap into the air. And soon the room was filled with kids singing, running, showing muscles, sticking out tongues.

"You're all important," pastor John shouted above the noise. "God needs you all."

And there, in the middle of the room, Elisha pulled out the scroll and wrote down, 'I am a part of God's body. Every part is important.'

She rolled it back up and put it into her bag. So she wasn't finished with the poem after all. Now she had to do it. She had to work with the others as one big body. She glanced down at a kid who was crawling past her, sniffing the floor as if he was a nose. It wasn't going to be easy.

"And what," she wondered, "What was about to fall under the table?"

17

One Body

Angela turned the cardboard box upside down and shook it several times. The last of the cereal was in her bowl, but there was no prize. “There’s nothing,” she said, almost in tears. “It’s not fair.”

Her mom looked at her dad with a worried expression. Her dad looked at Elisha. Elisha looked at Angela. It was true, it wasn’t fair.

Elisha went over to Angela and put her arm around her. “Let’s say a prayer,” she said.

“I don’t think we should pray about things like that,” her mom replied, brushing the crumbs off the table. “It would be rude to bother God. He’s far too busy to worry about such little things.”

“It’s not little,” Angela shouted, tears running down her face. “I’ve been waiting forever.”

Elisha remembered the prayer she had said, asking

God to help Angela find the prize, and her heart suddenly filled up with the warmth of the Holy Spirit, and the words that she spoke surprised all of her family, but most of all her. "God wants us to talk to him. And it's impossible for him to be too busy. Would you walk under a tree and ask the tree if it's too busy to shade you?"

Without any further discussion, all of her family held hands and prayed that Angela would find the gift. And even though the box appeared to be empty, nobody removed it from the middle of the kitchen table.

When Elisha arrived at school she saw Mark talking to Nicole. He was doing that shuffling thing with his feet again, and glancing down at the ground nervously. Elisha got closer, and he looked around and whispered, "Nicole asked me to come to the church youth group." The word 'church' was said especially quietly.

"Church group's great," Elisha said in a loud, cheerful voice.

Mark winced, and turned around to see if any of his usual friends had heard. They were far away on the opposite side of the room, playing a card game.

He turned back. "Sorry," he said. "It's just that they're into . . . other stuff."

On Sunday, all of the family were at the breakfast table except for Angela. Earlier in the week Angela had declared that she had "gone off breakfast," and "wasn't going to eat any more cereal." Her mom had suggested buying a plastic toy and sneaking it into the carton, and then pretending to find it. But Elisha had insisted that God wouldn't be happy with that plan, and they all just needed to have more faith, even if that meant never finding anything.

After that, nobody talked about the problem, and the box was left untouched. Nobody was talking much Sunday morning either, so when Angela suddenly came running into the room yelling "Yippee," the whole family jumped.

"God answered," she said, doing a little dance, then grabbing at the cereal box.

"He answered?" her dad questioned, looking confused. "How did he do that?"

"Well, he said it had been too early before, and that we'd eaten the cereal too fast." She paused adding, "Maybe it was all those ones I spilled on the table." Her face looked a little guilty, but she continued, "Anyway, he said that now it was the right time."

"He told you all that?" her dad said in a 'how can that happen' voice.

"Yep," Angela said, shaking the box extra hard now.

Elisha knew how it was. It was as if God put ideas into her heart, and then they traveled up to her mind to make long sentences.

"Maybe we should just throw the box away," her dad mumbled, when nothing appeared despite all the hard shaking.

Angela looked at him, determined. "Not until it comes out," she cried, and she started ripping at the cardboard. Long strips flew off onto the table, into the butter, into her dad's coffee, and her mom's toast. One side was completely ripped off, leaving only the inside bag where the cereals had been. Angela started on the other side. She tore a big piece.

"There," she shouted. She ripped again, and Elisha

saw that trapped between the bag and the box was a long, flat, golden packet. Angela gave one final rip and the packet flew out of the box, and under the table.

Elisha leapt up from her chair, "It's under the table. It's under the table," she shouted, pointing to the packet. "The thing under the table." Both she and her sister dived underneath, they bumped heads, and then Angela carefully and surprisingly slowly, picked it up.

Their mom and dad stayed sitting in their places, looking at all the mess, wondering if their children would ever be normal again.

Angela stood up and held the packet out. On the front was written "Mustard Seeds," and there was a picture of a bird sitting in the branches of a tree.

"Seeds," said Angela, in a voice that was as happy as if she had just been given a pony. "I've never had seeds." She stared at them a little longer, poked the packet with her finger, smelled it, and then her face became sad and she said, "I don't know how to grow them."

"I do," said Elisha. "I'll help you," and a rather surprised younger sister took Elisha's hand.

Angela was still holding onto Elisha and the seeds

when they got to church. "She can stay in the youth room with me," Elisha said to her mom, when Angela wouldn't let go.

Inside the room they saw Mark, and Nicole, and the other kids. Elisha was sure that the seed packet was the thing Angel Someone had talked about, but she didn't know why until Angela tapped on her arm and said, "I'm going to ask everyone if they will help plant the seeds."

"That's it," Elisha thought. "The group project." But then she looked around at the other kids. They were so much older than Angela, and they weren't interested in gardening. They liked computers, and music, and playing video games, and she turned back to tell her sister this, but Angela had already disappeared to the front of the room, and was climbing onto a table next to pastor John.

There was nothing she could do. Her poor sister would be embarrassed.

"Hello," Angela said, loud enough so everyone could hear. "I have some seeds, and we can all plant them around the church today."

She held the packet up, her small arm stretching high above their heads. Elisha cringed, ready for everyone to laugh, or worse yet, to ignore her completely.

Angela stretched her arm a little higher, and the gold of the packet caught the light. It began to glow brightly, shining in such a way that no matter where you stood, your eyes were naturally drawn towards it, like the star in the Kingdom of Nain. And once your eyes were on it, it was impossible to turn away, or to look at anything else. A hush fell over the room, and the normal twitching and fidgeting that usually went on, was stilled. And the longer everyone stood, the more they began to feel as if the brightness was now coming not only from the seeds, but also from inside themselves.

"Let's all plant the seeds," the boy now known as the mouth, shouted. Everyone cheered, and before Elisha could say anything, the group was opening the utility cupboards, and getting out spades and trowels. They formed a long line and marched into the church garden, with Elisha's sister, the smallest of all, too young really to even be in the youth room, leading with the golden packet in her hand.

Then they started to dig the soil, cut back bushes, move rocks of all sizes, and weed flower beds that hadn't been touched for months. Elisha watched for the birds, and the depth of the soil, and for distractions that might pull them from their task. But there were none, everyone was focused on the planting, and they became like one moving body, as if each belonged to the other. Arms pushed mowers, mouths gave suggestions, eyes looked for things needing to be done, and hands dug holes for planting. Everyone was working together, each person using their own special gift.

Pastor John helped to water the seeds, and Elisha carried a large jug of water around. She handed Mark a cup. "I never thought this could happen," Mark said, looking at everyone working.

Elisha smiled, "My sister was the one who brought the seeds."

"And asked the group," Mark added, in a quiet voice. He picked at a weed in the ground, tried to pull it out, but the root got stuck and the stem just broke in the middle. "I wish I was brave like that."

Elisha suddenly felt sad for him. She dug her trowel

under the root, and the plant popped out. "Maybe you just need more faith," she said.

Mark looked up at her suddenly, and she thought he was going to say something, something important, but then he just put his cup down, and went back to pulling up weeds. Elisha walked over to the next person, but then she turned and came back to Mark and said, "Sorry about all those underpants tickets."

Mark looked up again, smiling this time. "That's okay," he said, "Sometimes bad things turn out good."

When all the tasks were finished, they stood in the center of the garden, the seeds now under the earth, ready to grow, the plants and lawn perfectly trimmed, the weeds gone. And it felt to everyone standing there, as if they were exactly where they were supposed to be, that every leaf, plant, and even the tiny ladybugs with their black dotted bodies were just as God had planned. Elisha looked up at the sky, and thanked God for showing her that wonderful things happen when his helpers come together, and as she spoke to him she noticed that just above her, sitting in a tree, was the white dove from the clock tower.

It made a soft peaceful cooing sound. And Elisha knew that her work on the last scroll was complete.

18

The Meeting

Elisha tore open the large white envelope that arrived in the mail. Inside was an invitation from Nicole, and there was a picture of a tree like the ones in the church garden. Only this one was filled with the names of everyone who had helped with the planting of the mustard seeds. Stretching out across one of the branches was Elisha's name, along with Angela's and Mark's. At the top it said, 'Gardeners' Party.'

She had started out wanting to make God her best friend, but now she was making other friends too.

She picked up her Bible and scroll number five. Her heart told her it was time to put the scroll inside God's book, but she hesitated for a moment, feeling sad that her adventure was coming to an end. She stared out the window, watched the sun beginning to set, watched it slowly sink away.

Then just when the last of the orange slipped behind the horizon, and the long thin shadows of evening sank into the dark, she put the scroll inside her Bible and closed it.

It was day in the Kingdom of Nain. She was sitting at the edge of a river, and the water was flowing quickly, gushing over rocks as clear as crystals. The sound of bells rose from the river, and she leaned close to listen, and it seemed as if each wave of water made its own note as it passed over the rocks.

There was no Angel Someone or Angel Gabriel, only the music, and the river, and fruit trees like the ones she had planted. The golden one of faith, the liquid blue, and the red in the shape of a heart.

Elisha dipped her bare feet into the stream, and she felt the music tingling her toes, and then flowing through her body, like the river was becoming a part of her.

Anyone else sitting there might have worried that they were all alone. They might have looked around for the angels and the sheep, or nervously, impatiently, watched for others to appear. But Elisha felt none of these fears, and she knew without a doubt, without any doubt at all, that God was with her.

Then the great sound of trumpets shook the kingdom, and Elisha saw the golden lamb flying through the rainbows, wings spread out, reflecting the light.

It soared closer and closer, down from the sky until it landed right next to her. And all the kingdom was illuminated by its brightness, as if a piece of the sun had fallen to the earth.

Elisha stepped towards the lamb, stretched out her arm and touched its woolly head. Her fingers slipped through the soft curls and into its warmth. The lamb turned its face towards her, and she saw that its eyes were the color of the rich soil where the fruit trees had grown, and she felt as if this was the start of something wonderful, like a small seed being planted in the earth. And she became so focused on the lamb's eyes that she gave no attention to everything else around her, and she did not see that the lamb's body was fading, until the eyes disappeared too.

She jumped backwards, startled. The light became stronger, and she saw the outline of a tall figure standing where the lamb had been. Although she couldn't see the person clearly, because everything was now so very bright, she knew who it was immediately.

"Jesus," she shouted. He was there, next to her.

"Hello Elisha," he said.

"Hello God," she replied, as easily as talking to a

friend, a best friend. And she understood that he had always been there. He had always been next to her.

He reached out his arm, and she slipped her hand into his, and their fingers fit together perfectly. Then he lead her through the fruit trees, and along a path that wound up a mountain. She felt smooth pebbles under her feet, and she looked down and saw stones the color of sapphire. He picked one up and gave it to her. It was warm, and she dropped it into her pocket. They continued walking, up and up, until they arrived at the very top, and from there they could see the great valley, and the trees, and the river, and all the rainbows lined in a row.

The wind became stronger, and it lifted up her hair and blew the smell of flowers and fruit from the fields. She had never realized the kingdom was so large, that there were so many trees and plants. She suddenly felt very small compared to it all, like a tiny dot on a great map spread out before her.

And then, like the shadow inside Angel Someone, something inside her began to stir. But it wasn't a feeling of sadness, but of miraculous things to come. She turned her face towards the breeze, and closed her eyes. She held Jesus' hand tighter, and when she opened her eyes again she saw a large stretch of land to the right that she had never noticed before. It seemed to spread for miles, and as far as she could see there were bundles of straw sitting on what looked like cut fields of wheat. But there were also sections where the wheat had not been cut, where the wheat was so tall it bent over with the weight of the grain. It needed to be harvested too, but she couldn't see any angels, or farmers, or anyone helping. Was it just going to be left undone? Elisha didn't know why, but the sight of this land disturbed her greatly. Her heart gave a jump, like it wanted to fly towards the field, leap right off the mountain and go there, but instead she held onto the Lord as firmly as she could. Then suddenly he spoke.

"The kingdom," Jesus said, "needs gardeners. There is so much work to be done, but so few to do it."

And Elisha realized that he wasn't only talking about the Kingdom of Nain, but about the earth too. Tears of joy began to flow down her face. Jesus wanted help. He wanted her help. A great feeling of love rose up into her heart, and all she could say was, "Thank you." She was grateful that he would even ask.

Then they walked on further in silence until they came to the edge of the mountain. Elisha peered over the side and saw that it was very steep. At the bottom was rock as dark as night, and nothing was growing there. Nothing. She shuddered with the same cold feeling that had chilled her when she had met the pale man in the black coat and hat.

She stepped back from the edge, and she knew that the work Jesus wanted her to do was dangerous. And it wasn't just about plants, but about people. Jesus wanted her to help people. She took both of his hands in hers.

"I'm not afraid," she said, her voice loud and sure. "I'm not afraid with you by my side." And she felt strong and ready, and she said, "I'll be your helper. I'll be your gardener of plants and people too."

And her words floated out over the edge, and the cliff and the rocks vanished, and she found herself standing with Jesus in the middle of a rich green valley. There were trees, and the river, and the music like bells. In the distance she saw Angel Gabriel, and Angel Someone, and the sheep.

She waved to them and they waved back. Then the bells from the river changed to the sound of voices singing. Jesus raised his hands, and the song became louder, coming not only from the river, but from the fields, and the sky. Then more angels appeared, and the song they sang said that nothing could separate her from the love of God that is in Jesus. Nothing. Not life, nor death, nor present, or future, or any powers, or anything in all creation. Nothing. Jesus' love for her was greater than all these things.

And Elisha sensed that the kingdom was about to disappear, and she tightened her grip on Jesus' hand, as if trying to keep him near. Then she laughed at how silly that was. He would be with her. Always.

19

The Beginning

Elisha opened her eyes to the early morning sunlight. God's light. In the distance she saw a rainbow, and she had the feeling that Angel Gabriel must have put it there. She looked down at the table next to her bed, and she saw the smooth sapphire pebble that Jesus had given her. She picked it up, and held it in her hands. It felt warm, comforting.

She looked out of the window. It was strange, but she had never noticed before how green the trees were, how the sky was painted such bright colors, how many of the birds sang in the garden. It felt as if she was waking up for the very first time in her life, like she had been asleep for years and years.

Then she remembered the widow in Nain. Is this what her son felt like when Jesus brought him back to life? Like he had been asleep? She got up. Night was over. Day was here.

She was now a child of God. And her journey was just beginning.

About the Author

Christine Lê grew up in England and the United States. She has a Ph.D. in counseling psychology from New York University, and presently works as a licensed psychologist with children and adults in schools, private practice, and a clinic for Down Syndrome.

She has received awards and grants for her writing from the Ludwig Vogelstein Foundation, the Windward Arts Council, and the National League of American Pen Women. She has spoken on writing and faith in schools, churches, and professional groups.

Her first book, *The Hawai'i Snowman*, a fully illustrated Christmas tale, was #1 on the bestseller list in Hawai'i. Available on Amazon.

About the illustrator

Michel Lê is an award winning illustrator and graphic designer who grew up in France. After working in Paris, London, New York and Honolulu, he is now an art director for an advertising agency in Birmingham, Alabama.

Kingdom of Nain is Michel's and Christine's second book collaboration. Their first book, *The Hawai'i Snowman,* won the top award for book design.

Michel and Christine live with their two daughters in Homewood, Alabama. They are members of Fullness Christian Fellowship church.

Made in the USA
Lexington, KY
19 February 2015